DON'T FORGET THE

BUTTERFLIES

DON'T FORGET THE BUTTERFLIES

A Love Story

by

Lynn G. Armstrong

Text © 2023 by Lynn G. Armstrong
All rights reserved.

ISBN: 979-8-9893042-4-0

Printed in the United States of America

DEDICATION

To Jim Armstrong, my soulmate, and best friend who taught me the real meaning of love, and to all the Vietnam veterans who lost their lives defending our country. We can never forget.

The Butterfly

I sleep safe and protected in my cocoon.
A keeper of dreams
One day, I awaken.
Wings wet, and trembling with joy
I soar, the sky is my canvas,
The wind, my navigator
I light on a flower before you.
You stare.
The light reflects my radiance.
I am life.
On my wings, I carry your dreams.
Come follow me, I whisper.
The journey awaits.
You smile and shake your head.
I fly away.
You stare.
Your eyes are wet with dreams that could have been.

LGA 2010

ACKNOWLEDGEMENTS

Thanks to Cheri Sullenberger, LCSW, who took the time out of her busy schedule to let me interview her.

Thanks to Sylvie Kurtz, my instructor from Longridge Writers Group College, who put in the extra time and effort to push me.

Thanks to all my readers of *Murder by Definition,* my first novel, who have motivated me to keep writing with their kind words.

As always, thanks to my family and friends who continue to support me in my writing and art. It never goes unnoticed.

PROLOGUE

Edie Carrington staggered back to her bed after returning from a routine trip to the bathroom and felt herself slowly slide into that wonderful sleep zone we all covet. Suddenly, she jolted wide awake. Now what? What was that? There it was again. A loud thud and then another. Was it Beacon, that silly dog? No, she could hear him barking, but it didn't sound like it was coming from outside.

She padded down the hall, not even looking for her slippers. This had better be good. "Oh, dear God!" Directly in front of her, Aaron was on all fours in front of the kitchen cabinets only in his shorts and a T-shirt; his head and body rocking back and forth in an undulating trancelike motion as he repeatedly slammed his head into the cabinets with a loud bang over and over. She hurried around to face him as he continued to slam his head against the cabinets. Only blank eyes stared back at her, and he was oblivious to her or his surroundings. "Aaron, for God's sake, STOP," she pleaded. "You'll hurt yourself!" Her pleas fell on deaf ears. Beacon was barking nonstop. She raced to the phone and called an ambulance. It took two EMTs to hold him down to give him an injection to sedate him enough; to be able to get him on a stretcher and into the ambulance. He was fighting as if his life depended on it but still seemed to be out of it and mumbling incoherently.

Chapter One

The Seventies

"Edie Carrington, I am delighted to meet you finally. I'm Dr. Trent, your sister's psychiatrist," he said, offering his hand. "Welcome to Averton. I am one of your most devoted fans. I have every one of your records. Can I get you a cup of coffee? I know you've been looking for your sister for a long time and are anxious to see her once again, but I feel I should prepare you. Twelve years is a long time. Amy has come a long way but still has a long way to go. When she first arrived at Averton, your sister couldn't respond to any external stimuli. While she wasn't catatonic, she seemed incapable of any emotional response and operated strictly on verbal command.

"How did she get here? How did you know where to find me? She's been missing for so long I wasn't sure I'd ever find her. I didn't even know if she was alive. I even hired a private detective to look for her. The closest I ever got to a lead was, the detective said he had a tip she was seen in Alabama a few years ago, and then there was nothing."

"She was brought here by the police, but a neighbor recognized her at the police station of all places. It seems your sister was attacked by someone and beaten pretty badly. The night they brought her in, witnesses saw her wandering around disoriented and confused for hours, not too far from her apartment. A concerned citizen brought her to the police station. When they performed a rape kit on her, the nurse on duty that night determined she was sexually assaulted. Mr. Canton, a neighbor just happened to be at the station for an unrelated matter to see if he could identify a suspect in a lineup as the burglar that broke into his store. He saw your sister as he was leaving and recognized her immediately. The rape may have been the trigger that caused her to have a breakdown. That is all the information I have right now. Mr. Canton said the only relative he knew of was a sister she'd mentioned to him a few times. Her landlord has been a big help too. Of course, with your reputation as a singer and fan base, it wasn't difficult to track you down after that."

"Dear God, will she recognize me? Does she have a clue what has happened to her?"

"I'm not sure. She is non-responsive right now so asking her anything is going down a blind alley. If we're lucky, seeing you could be the catalyst that brings her back. As I said, twelve years is a long time. I'm just not sure if she'll be able to make the emotional connection you're accustomed to. Considering what I've been able to piece together you girls endured as children, it is a miracle you haven't suffered a similar fate yourself. It's obvious that

2

you've been able to externalize some of your pain throughout your career. Amy's breakdown didn't happen overnight. Whatever her memories are, she has chosen to escape for now. Amy still feels she is responsible for you as well as herself but is all over the place as far as reality goes. One minute she's talking as an adult, and the next she is reliving her childhood when you were little girls. Other days she may go the whole day as if she is in a trance and never say a word.

"What can I do? I'd be glad to fill in the blanks for you or help in any way I can. Sometimes when I'm on tour, it may have to be by phone. Just let me know."

"Thank you. I'll certainly take you up on that. Come with me, I'll walk you to her room."

Edie was surprised to see Amy's psychiatrist was her age or at least close to it. While Dr. Trent was just under six feet, his demeanor and carriage implied a much taller man. He was a handsome man with a full head of blond curly hair and electric blue eyes. She noticed he ran his hands through his hair and frowned when he was concentrating. This may have accounted for the start of a barely perceptible receding hairline.

As Edie walked to her sister's room with Dr. Trent, she realized someone had studied color and its effect on emotions as she admired the pale peach walls up and down the long hall. Out of nowhere, her thoughts were immediately hijacked to when she and Amy were growing up.

***

"Mother, you did it again. You've painted me with blue eyes. My eyes are green." It would be years before she made the connection from her mother's rage to her father's green eyes.

"Do not speak to me in that tone, young lady. You will answer me with respect at all times, do you understand me?"

3

"Yes, Mother."

Edie's mother, Olivia Carrington Martin, was a well-known artist able to supplement her current secretarial position with enough income to raise her two daughters in between husbands. Edie and Amy were devastated when their parents split up. Edie was only four years old, but it was daunting now that Amy was a teenager and Edie was five years behind her. Sometimes, Edie felt like there was a constant influx of men every time she turned around. Each time her mother met someone new, their lives changed all over again. Her mother seemed to have an attraction for men in uniform. Because of it, Amy and Edie were always leaving friends behind every time they moved, courtesy of the military. In another town, another school became their norm. Years later, Edie wasn't sure which one her mother married because no one seemed to stay long, and they moved a lot.

"Mother, I don't want to go to school. I'm sick." Edie said.

"You're not sick, you're neurotic. Of course, you have managed to work yourself into a frenzy again. Throwing up is a result, not a symptom. Get your jacket, or you will miss the bus. You will feel better when you get your mind busy and stop feeling sorry for yourself. Are you bawling again? Stop it right now, or I swear I'm going to take you to a psychiatrist." For some reason this terrified Edie, even though she never knew anyone in their family who had gone to a psychiatrist. Her mother must have known how it freaked her out because she threatened Edie with taking her to a psychiatrist regularly or whenever she got upset. It would never occur to her mother to take time out and console her daughter or find out what had upset her in the first place. Edie would be a grown woman before she realized it was just another way her mother could use fear to control her emotionally.

Edie was so angry with her mother that she felt like she couldn't breathe and fought the nausea all the way to the bus stop.

"Quit mumbling Edie, I'm nervous too," Amy said. "I hate the first day in a new school. One good thing is we get to make new friends. Maybe it will help you get over your shyness. At least we have each other." Grabbing Edie, she gave her a quick hug, before the bus arrived. Amy was five years older than her sister and most of the time found her to be a royal pain but worried about her and was always in the background watching out for her.

Edie's stomach finally settled down by the time the bus arrived. Amy always had that effect on her.

When they got off the bus, Amy walked Edie toward her room, hugged her, and hurried off to make it to her classroom before the bell rang.

Edie noticed the strap of one of her shoes had come undone and squatted down to fix it when she thought she heard her name. That's when she realized two teachers were whispering about her.

"Isn't that Edie Carrington, the new student? Can you believe she's not even wearing a slip? You can see right through that dress. Who lets their little girl go out the door like that let alone come to school half-dressed?"

"I'm not surprised, she and her sister were in foster care for three years. It seems the stepmother didn't want them. What kind of father gives his children up for a woman? They're back with their mother now and have a brand-new stepfather. I heard this is stepfather number two since the divorce if she was even married to the first one. Their biological father registered them last week. So sad, they don't seem to have any continuity in their lives, do they? What a shame."

Edie was horrified. How could they talk about her like that and how did they know so much about her? She was mortified. When she finished buckling her shoe and stood up, they must have realized she heard them because the teacher who was clucking about her not wearing a slip, turned red in the face and took off. Her mother made the dress for her first day at the new school and Edie was actively arguing with her before she left and completely forgot to put on a slip. It was a silky material and Edie was so proud of it. Olivia Carrington Martin, her mother, was an excellent seamstress. She and Amy recently moved back in with their mother and stepfather, so she was thrilled her mother had made it for her. Now she hated it and knew she would never wear it again. She walked into her new classroom, head down, wishing she could just disappear and magically be home.

"Class, we have a new student today. Edie Carrington is with us all the way from Arizona. Edie, you may take a seat."

"Not by me you won't, four eyes," a boy said as she walked to the empty seat behind him and sat down.

"Eric Hoffman, you may go directly to the principal's office and don't even think of coming back until you are ready to apologize to Edie." Edie ignored him when he turned around and stuck his tongue out at her before he sulked off.

***

"Amy, someone is here to see you."

Catching her breath, Edie found it impossible to believe this woman in front of her was her sister. It was hard to recognize this strange person with her shoulders slumped, head down, and her face partially covered by what remained of her lustrous and shoulder-length hair. Stringy, thin, and dull hair was a sad substitute for what used to be Amy's crowning glory.

Suddenly, Edie was propelled back in time again. She was fifteen and her mother was in one of her crazy moods.

"Edie come here. Sit down." Her mother was standing in the dining room with her hands on her hips and a package of boxed hair color was sitting on the dining room table. Edie sat down with reluctance and dread. Her mother grabbed a towel from the table, and put it around Edie's shoulders, and clipped it with a clothespin.

"What are you doing?" Edie asked, pulling the towel off, and putting it on the chair beside her. The clothespin flew off and landed on the floor.

"I'm going to make you a blonde. I'm sick and tired of hearing you whine you wished you were a blonde."

"But I never said I wanted to be a blonde." Edie jumped up, grabbed the towel off the back of the chair, and threw it on the floor. Her mother promptly ignored her, picked up the towel, and pushed her down in the chair by her shoulders, put the towel around her shoulders again, and clipped it with another clothespin she pulled from her pocket. Her mother was in what she and Amy called her "psycho mood." By now, Edie was crying and knew if she got up again or persisted it would be worse for her. Only God knew how crazy her mother could get.

Fortunately, her hair was so dark, or her mother had no idea what she was doing because it only brought out the red in her hair and the result was a pretty auburn-streaked effect like she had spent some time in the sun. Afterward, when she pulled herself together and looked in the mirror, she realized she liked it but hid her feelings as she was afraid her mother would do something worse if she thought she liked it. The only problem was when her roots started to grow out her mother refused to give her the money to let her touch it up. She had to live with it for months as her hair was so long. Eventually, she cut it herself to get rid of the bleached ends and caught hell for it, but at least she didn't look like a freak.

***

7

Chapter Two

Edie leaned over and cupped Amy's chin in both hands, lifting her sister's face to meet her own.

"Amy, I'm here." A face with two holes burned into it for eyes looked back at her. For a split second, a spark of recognition flashed across her face and then it was gone.

"What time is it? I need to pick up Dad. We're supposed to have lunch today at Bentley's." Before Edie could come up with an answer, Amy was staring off into space once again, oblivious to her surroundings.

Edie looked at Dr. Trent and noticed his eyebrows furrow together. It was obvious he was aware their dad and stepmother had died in a terrible car accident years ago.

"This happens sometimes. Your sister seems to be having a trying day. It is easier sometimes to drift in and out of reality than to fight it. The good news is it isn't permanent."

"Maybe you girls could go outside for a while. It's a gorgeous day and the grounds here are beautiful; a great escape for our patients and their families."

"That sounds wonderful! Amy loves the outdoors. Amy, would you like to go outside for a while?" Edie's request fell on deaf ears and Amy's facial expression was that of someone in a trance. Edie picked up her sister's hand from the chair arm and Amy rose from her chair like an automaton when Edie gently squeezed her hand. Amy let her sister lead her like an innocent child.

Edie was pleasantly surprised when she saw the beautiful, maintained grounds of Averton Psychiatric Hospital. She chose to sit with her sister on an inviting bench that overlooked a large pond enjoyed by a half dozen ducks and at least that many baby ducklings. She noticed there were five other benches placed around the circular pond. Four were empty but the one closest on their right was occupied by an attractive thirtyish appearing man, with a handsome profile staring into space, and a magnificent golden retriever quietly sitting at his feet. Whatever was in his visual range, it was obvious he wasn't looking at it. It puzzled her and she couldn't help wondering what his story was. Was he depressed? He was at a psychiatric hospital after all. They sat for a while. Edie talked to her sister, not knowing if she even heard her but hoping that something would get through to her. It had been years but now that she'd found her sister, Edie planned to visit her as often as she could and hoped one day, Amy would find her way back from the emotional prison she was in and be able to leave. "Come on Amy let's go for a walk." She stood up and pulled Amy to her feet, looping her arm into hers, and they walked around the grounds. They stopped at a lovely gazebo, open on the front and back with generous flowerbeds on each side, rich with flowers of every color and shape imaginable. While they sat on the bench inside the gazebo, the floral perfume from the flowerbeds filled their nostrils. During all of this, her sister only moved when Edie moved, allowing herself to be led anywhere she was taken but otherwise oblivious to Edie or the beautiful grounds that surrounded them. As they left the gazebo behind and walked past the pond, they passed behind the young man again. He was still sitting on the bench staring off into space and his magnificent dog was obediently sitting at his feet. As they got closer, the man jumped up like a shot and whirled around to face them.

"Hello, who's there?"

"I'm sorry. We didn't mean to startle you," Edie said. "I'm just here visiting my sister." He was tall, well over six feet with dark, almost black wavy hair and beautiful blue eyes that stared right through her and a deep sadness that covered him like a shroud. Edie was shaken as she led Amy away. She immediately realized this handsome man who looked like he spent many hours a week in a gym, was blind. The beautiful creature next to him who never left his side to explore his surroundings like most dogs would, must be his service dog. How could she have missed it? She still wondered what his story was and why he was at Averton.

Aaron Weissman could feel the sun on his face and enjoyed the sounds of spring all around him. Spring used to be his favorite season of the year. The woman's melodious voice and perfume still clung to the air after they passed by his bench. He listened to the woman speaking to someone in a soft voice, but no one answered her. Then he couldn't hear anything. Suddenly, he felt even lonelier than usual. Beacon, his dog whimpered with empathy, and he patted him on his head.

"Beacon, my boy, I'm all right, thanks to you."

***

Manchon Hospital

"Aaron, I'm Dr. Falcon; welcome to Manchon. I want you to stop worrying and assure you, once the swelling behind your eyes recedes you will be as good as new. We haven't even removed the bandages yet. Right now, we need to get you out of that bed so you can join the living again," Dr. Falcon said. "I've assigned a nurse to you who can facilitate that. Ms. Aleen has been nursing our boys back to health for a long time. You're in excellent hands. I expect to hear great things from Ms. Aleen soon on your progress." Patting him on the foot, he walked out the door filling Aaron with a debilitating feeling of loneliness and helplessness.

"Okay Aaron, it's a beautiful day. Let's see what's going on," Dr. Falcon said, closing the blinds and drawing the curtain around Aaron's bed. "I know you must be anxious to get home and get on with your life. Your accident has given you a nice little vacation from Charlie, you know until you've finished healing."

As Dr. Falcon carefully unwrapped Aaron's bandages, Aaron kept his eyes closed the whole time.

"All right Aaron, open your eyes. Take it slow. The light can be brutal at first."

Fortunately, the light didn't bother his eyes at all. Unfortunately, he couldn't see anything. He was completely blind.

"Oh my, I wasn't expecting this at all. Don't panic Aaron, we'll run some more tests and get to the bottom of this" After a battery of tests that dragged on for three days and waiting another nail-biting two days for the results, the verdict was the same. Aaron was blind.

"Aaron, I am so sorry. According to your test results, there is no physical reason why you shouldn't be able to see. It's a medical conundrum."

"Are you saying this is all in my mind or I'm faking it so I can get out on a medical discharge?"

"Of course not. I am going to get you out of that bed and order some physical therapy for you right away. It will help your frame of mind. This is devastating news, but you can't give up. We'll get to the bottom of it. You have my word."

After smashing most of the few things he had on his nightstand, Aaron cried until his eyes were sore and swollen. He was in a large men's ward whose victims suffered from various injuries from the war but for the present, he could only focus on himself. He had no privacy, with all the people and noise from the ward but he'd never felt more alone in his life.

"Mr. Weissman, good morning. I'm Katherine Aleen, your nurse. We'll be spending a lot of time together in the next few weeks or longer. How well you progress is completely up to you."

The last thing Aaron wanted to do was listen to some bubbly airhead nurse who must have been behind the door when God passed out voices. Besides sounding like she had a mouthful of gravel, she rattled on incessantly about absolutely nothing. Katherine Aleen could put Chatty Kathy to shame. His head felt like it would explode any minute. He had just been given the worst news of his young life and was barely hanging on emotionally. Now he was lying flat on his back in Manchon, a military hospital 100 miles just outside of the war zone in Vietnam that had robbed him of his sight.

"Aaron, I hope it's all right to call you that. I have a surprise for you. Here at Manchon, we are fortunate enough to have Spirit Angels, a service dog farm, we work closely with nearby, and it seems your father has decided if you had a service dog to work with, he would not only be good company for you but give you a jump start on your healing. He must love you a great deal. Meet Trip, your new best friend. Trip, this is Aaron Weissman." Trip greeted his new friend with a soft grunt.

Aaron felt a wet tongue lick his hand, reached out and felt the softest fur he ever remembered, and stroked him on his head. He could feel the tears roll down his face. "I'm sorry buddy, but they've assigned you to the wrong person." The sweet golden retriever proceeded to wash the tears from Aaron's face as if to let him know he felt his pain.

"Aaron, these dogs, are selected from the time they are puppies and trained for months by their handlers to fulfill the mission they were born for," she rattled on ignoring his emotional state. "You're extremely fortunate your dad has given you such a special gift. Tomorrow you will meet Trip's handler and the three of you will begin training together. You're a lucky young man. Spirit Angels is a top-of-the-line service dog farm and not everyone can afford these beautiful creatures." Aaron got a quick kiss on the cheek from Trip before Katherine turned around and led him out; he could hear the sound of Trip's footpads getting lighter and lighter as he left his room and padded down the hall.

The next morning, he awoke to Katherine's prattling and Trip's rubbing against his hand. "It's time to get out of that bed, Aaron," He could hear her pulling up the window shade by his bed. It sure couldn't be for his benefit. What was there for him to see anyway? All he wanted to do was to go back to sleep and be left alone. "It's a brand-new day and we have lots to do." Aaron could hear the wheelchair wheels as she spun it around and he sat up in the bed. Trip barked and pushed his cold nose against Aaron's hand. "Bossy fella, aren't you?" Aaron responded by sitting down in the wheelchair and garnered a friendly grunt and an instant look of approval from Trip which of course he couldn't see.

"Trip and I will be back in a little while to get you. Your orderly is here to take you to the shower room, and he'll buzz us as soon as you're done. Be ready to start work ASAP." Katherine Aleen reminded Aaron of an old drill sergeant he had once in basic training.

DON'T FORGET THE BUTTERFLIES

Chapter Three

"Here we are. Aaron. I'd like you to meet Cal Forester, Trip's handler, and trainer until he is officially turned over to you. The three of you will become a team working for the same goal."

The days flew by, much to Aaron's surprise, and falling in love with Trip was something he had no control over from the very beginning. The two of them were never apart. Trip slept on his own pad on the floor by Aaron's bed and anticipated his every move. Once, Aaron rolled over in his sleep and was too close to the edge. He would have fallen off, but Trip body blocked him and barked until Aaron could reposition himself in the bed. When a nurse came running, Aaron said. "No problem here, we've got everything under control, right Trip?" Trip proved to be quite the taskmaster and had a special bark to encourage him whenever Aaron wanted to throw his hands up and quit. Aaron couldn't believe how intelligent this seventy-five pounds of golden fur beauty he could only imagine looked, was, and was always ready to encourage his beloved Aaron. One day in particular, Aaron slammed into something for the third time and was beyond frustrated and fired off a string of obscenities that would make a sailor blush. Trip sensed his every emotion and immediately grabbed Aaron's sleeve and walked under his hand until Aaron could feel the lead on his harness as if to say, "We are a team and I'll help if you'll just let me." That was a turning point for Aaron, and he soon learned how Trip guided him by changing his response to Aaron's lead. If Trip knew they were too close to an object he would gently pull to the left or right. When there was imminent danger ahead, he immediately sat down and applied pressure to Aaron's knee so he would stop as well.

"You know what Trip, you are like a beautiful beacon of light that guides me to safety, and we have become a team. From now on you are Beacon to me. What do you think, would you like to be my Beacon?" Trip's answer was a special bark and he looked with adoration at Aaron as if he understood. "I'll take that as a yes, young man." From then on, Trip responded immediately to Beacon as if it was the only name he'd ever known.

At last, Aaron and Beacon, his service dog, were finally back in the States at Averton Psychiatric Hospital, and Dr. Trent, his psychiatrist's diagnosis of "hysterical blindness, "was in complete agreement with his doctors in Manchon. In his mind he understood, but try as he did many times, he was unable to physically force himself to see. It just wasn't going to happen. At first, his memory was foggy, but he was told when he woke up at Manchon Hospital that an explosive land mine had gone off three hundred feet from him in the Vietnam jungle. His best friend, Hank was killed immediately when he tripped over a tree root and fell face down on a land mine. They had gone through basic training together and every mission after that. It should have been him. He had so much guilt. Their unit was on a maneuver and the area was dense as usual. He was behind Hank, clearing the thick shrubbery so prevalent in the Vietnam jungle with his KA-BAR. He stopped to relieve his bladder and realized he'd left his KA-BAR behind. Initially, the last thing he remembered was when he went back to look for it. Everything else was a blank. He didn't remember the explosion or anything else until he woke up in Manchon Hospital. When they told him about Hank, he was emotionally shattered. Part of his head and eyes were covered in bandages, so he didn't know he was blind until they took the bandages off. At first, the doctors assured him there was nothing to panic about. They believed he would be fine when the swelling went down, but nothing happened. Dr. Trent, his psychiatrist at Averton Psychiatric Hospital said he suffered from survival guilt, and his "hysterical blindness," was a direct result of it. Great, it wasn't rocket science. In his mind, he knew there was nothing he could have done. If he hadn't stopped to use the bathroom it could have been both of them. He missed his friend, and he got it, but he still couldn't see a damn thing. Dr. Falcon, from the hospital he stayed at immediately after the accident in Vietnam, was optimistic at first but didn't waste any time delivering the cold hard facts as soon as they removed the bandages. Thank God for Beacon, his dedicated service dog and now devoted companion. He still couldn't believe his dad had purchased Beacon from Spirit Angels for him. It touched his heart. Spirit Angels was a nearby canine farm just outside the military combat zone that raised and trained canines as service dogs for those who had special needs from the war for whatever reason. They bonded immediately as soon as he and Beacon started training together. He was slowly finding his way back emotionally when he was notified his parents were killed in a plane crash before he even made it home. They were on a vacation in the Hawaiian Islands and were on their way home when their plane went down. It was such a shock losing both of them so suddenly. He didn't even get to go to their funeral. He was an emotional wreck. Dr. Falcon was worried about him. He and his dad didn't always agree on everything, but they were remarkably close. As strong as his dad was, his mother with all her elegance and intellect, was the force behind them all. He felt as if the ground had been pulled out from under him and more alone than he had ever been in his entire life.

***

Reflecting even farther back, he could recall a more pleasant time when the only thing Aaron Weissman, Caleb Rushing, and Tom Prentis had in common was their friendship. His parents were still living at the time. Aaron and Caleb were students at OU in Norman, Oklahoma. Tom previously flunked out and was going to give it another try. Somehow, they all managed to be overlooked by the draft. Their mantra was always, "Make love, not war."

Aaron was in his fourth year at OU with a brilliant medical future ahead of him. Vietnam held no attraction for him but his hours at flight school held him spellbound. When he was in the air behind the controls, he felt such exhilaration, he was as hooked as any addict waiting for his next fix. He knew when he got his wings, it was a given he would wind up in Vietnam, but flying was his mistress, and she was a jealous and consuming lover. There was always a shortage of pilots. Whatever it took to keep flying was Aaron's only focus. He worried how he would manage to juggle flight school with college, but he'd pull it off somehow. If he did go to Vietnam, he would be a third generation of sons to serve his country. Maybe that would pacify his dad.

"Aaron, why is this the first I've heard about you signing up for flight school?" David Weissman asked. "Are you planning on going to Vietnam as well?"

"Dad, it's almost a given when I graduate from flight school. The army is desperate for pilots. I thought you would be proud of me since I would be a third generation Weissman to fight for his country."

"Of course, I'm proud of you son but what about school; your medical career? Do you know why there's a shortage of pilots? Because a high percentage of pilots get shot down." It was easy to see where Aaron got his good looks. David Weissman was a force of a man who caused heads to turn whenever he entered a room. It wasn't just his dark curly hair that never stayed put or his 6'3" statuesque frame and broad shoulders. It was the force of the man and how he effortlessly commanded respect wherever he went. "I just assumed school would always come first. It's not like you can't serve your country at any time. First things first, right? By that time maybe the war will be over, and you can serve your country another way besides getting your ass shot off. You are a government issue to the army and therefore expendable." He wanted to stand by his son and never intended to mention his concerns or scare him to death, but he was desperate and hoped Aaron would change his mind.

"Dad, I love flying and I don't see any reason why I can't do both. It might be a challenge at times but I'm young and single, so I don't have to answer to anyone but myself right now. Come on, Dad, let's go to lunch. I'll pick up the tab."

"Aaron, are you crazy, man? You know flight school will guarantee you a one-way ticket to Vietnam." Caleb said.

"I know Caleb. You too? You sound like my dad. Worst case scenario, I might have to shelve school for a while. I can always pick it back up on the GI plan."

Caleb had no desire to go to Vietnam and couldn't understand his friend Aaron at all. Caleb Rushing was a heartbreaker and was in college strictly for the girls. His GPA left little doubt where his focus was.

Tom Prentis was born and raised in Norman, Oklahoma with everything going for him. His parents were in the cattle business and independently wealthy. Tom was their only child, so they had no one else to lavish their luxury on. Flunking out of school, two semesters in a row, was just one of a lengthy line of antics that kept his parents breathing down Tom's neck and busy cleaning up his messes. Among other things, they managed to keep Tom out of Vietnam by calling in a favor and getting Tom's medical records to include a hearing loss in one ear. Neither one of his college buddies was a good influence on Aaron. He definitely was busy sowing his wild oats. It was a miracle he managed somehow to keep up his grades and stay on the dean's list.

"Caleb, what the hell, get it together," Aaron hissed through clenched teeth. "I'm as drunk as you are, you fool, but at least I've still got my clothes on, and can walk. I hope she was worth it. Where in the hell is Tom? It sure is dark out here. I wonder who the fool was that shot out the streetlights? If it weren't for your pearly whites and your white ass, I never would have been able to see you. I don't know how long the batteries are going to last in my flashlight. Do you realize it's three in the morning, you idiot? How long have you been out here? You can't sleep out here in a planter for cripes sake; you'll be expelled. When did you get so fat? A little help here would be nice, you know. I'm doing all the work," He groaned. He pulled and pulled until Caleb finally slid out the rest of the way from the planter naked as the day he was born. "You're disgusting, man." It took them both three times to fall down the last level of five steps to their dorm to finally make it to their rooms. The rest of the day neither one of them could make it to class. They were in so much pain from all their bruises, in addition to Caleb's ant bites from the planter. Caleb made Aaron swear on his life no one would ever know he wore pink Calamine lotion on his butt and no briefs for a week. Luckily, it was Friday, and they had the weekend to rest. Unfortunately, there was no hope for the peonies that Caleb used for a temporary mattress in the huge planter. Those were the days.

***

Edie was just getting off a long tour of five cities, including New Orleans. It was a grueling trip, and she was exhausted. She grabbed the first flight she could get back to Atlanta and to Averton to see Amy. Her mind drifted back to when she and Amy were little girls.

Chapter Four

The Skating Rink

Edie gave herself up to the euphoria that embraced her as her long, dark, silky hair fanned around her young face, her five-year-old frame in perfect symmetry and balance as she skated. Round and round, she twirled on her long legs, her skates barely touching the ground. She could feel everyone watching her and it was intoxicating. The massive roller-skating rink was at the very bottom of a bowl-like structure. It was an especially special attraction for people to sit on the bleachers and enjoy the skaters below. It was exceptionally beautiful at night with its elaborate and romantic lighting and never failed to attract a crowd. Her energy was limitless; she knew she could do anything. She was too young to process the exhilaration she felt. All she knew was she loved the attention she got when others were watching her. She knew she would grow up and be on a stage with lots of adoring fans. She would be a singer. Her dad called it "a little girl's fantasy." Was this what it felt like when the crowd loved you?

"Look at me, Amy! Look at me! I'm skating. I can go so fast I could fly if I wanted to."

"I'm looking at you Edie, so what? You can't fly. That's stupid. Come on, Daddy is ready to go home now," she said looking up. She saw him standing among the sea of bleachers waving, directly above them. "Let's go."

"Is Momma coming?"

"No, she's not. We don't have a momma. Mommas care about their children. She doesn't care about us."

Edie pulled away from her sister with a vengeance, tears streaming down her face, threw herself down on the nearest bench, and pulled her skates off as fast as her small hands would move.

"I don't believe you. I want my momma." she wailed. Edie, sullen, and eyes downcast, allowed her sister to take her hand and lead her away from her beloved skating rink.

Edie idolized her older sister, Amy, but she wanted her mother. A five-year-old didn't understand the concept of divorce or why she and her sister were with their father and stepmother. Amy was furious at their mother, and it baffled Edie.

"Hi Daddy," Edie said. Her face glowed. "Are we going for ice cream?"

Martin swung his little girl up in the air and looked up at her sad eyes with a heavy heart. "I'm sorry sweetheart, not today. Caroline is preparing supper. She wouldn't want you girls to spoil your appetite."

Martin felt so guilty. How could he explain divorce to a five-year-old and a ten-year-old? He was extremely tired of their mother's escapades. It was obvious she was morally irresponsible and had a thing for men in uniform. They were less than a mile from a military base. When he came home one night from a night shift, he couldn't believe the girls were by themselves. He discovered later from neighbors, that she was frequenting a local nightclub close to the military base and staying there until it closed. He made it clear it better not happen again, but it proved to be an exercise in futility. He started checking with more of their neighbors and it seemed the girls had been left alone many times with Amy in charge. Martin was incredulous when he discovered his girls by themselves one night again when he was working late, and he told Olivia he wanted a divorce. What did she expect? He suspected she was sleeping around for months but this was the final *coup de grace*. He knew the girls would be devastated by the divorce, but their safety was his first priority. He would find a way to help his girls deal with the aftermath somehow. At least they would be safe. He hoped Caroline would warm up to his children soon and they could provide a healthy and loving environment for them.

***

Edie was visiting her mother one weekend and heard some movement in the little den which was more like a library with all its books. Her dad was letting her mother stay in the old house until she could find somewhere else to live. She knew her mother often loved to escape there sometimes and sit in her favorite overstuffed chair and read for hours. The den was dark, so she was surprised to hear a man's voice she didn't recognize coming from the couch in the little den.

"Hello, you must be Edie. I'm Edwin. You are a pretty little thing, aren't you? How old are you?"

"Five," Edie said. At the same time, she held up five fingers to show the man lying on her mother's couch. She often did this so she wouldn't have to talk when she was feeling shy and something about this stranger made her feel uncomfortable.

"Why don't you come here and sit with me for a while, and we can get to know each other a little better? I always wanted a little girl like you." He said, patting the space next to him.

"No, thank you."

"So, you can talk after all. I bet you would sit with your daddy." At that, Edie took off to find her mother hoping she'd never hear from this strange man lurking in the dark again. She decided immediately she didn't like him. Little did she know that her mother's new friend would one day be her stepfather. And that was how it started. The chase would go on for years; her stepfather after her and her mother would show up just in time to run Edie off and scold her for bothering him as if it was her fault. Edie couldn't understand her mother's anger or her own fear of her stepfather and learned right away to avoid him every chance she got. However, it would be three years before she had to cross that bridge. Since her father had custody of the girls, they only saw their mother on the weekends. That was a bone of contention for Caroline, however. If it were left up to her, they would be out of the picture altogether.

"Martin, when are you going to get it? Have you noticed your daughter at all lately? It looks like Edie has been dressing herself. She's falling apart. Have you seen her hair? It's probably not been combed since you dropped her off Friday. What will people think?"

"Caroline, the child is old enough to dress herself, and I could care less what other people think. Give her a break and time to learn. She's been through a lot in her young life. Maybe you could help her and give her some pointers from a stepmother's perspective."

"Pointers, you must be kidding," Caroline said. Her face was scarlet and a vein in her neck looked like it would pop any minute. "She is not my child and I never signed up to raise another woman's children. It's quite simple, Martin. You have a choice to make. It's either them or me."

"You can't be serious."

"Them or me."

"Very well, I'll put the girls with the Crain's again for a few weeks until I can decide what to do." At the time of Martin's divorce, when he first reported to the court his children were abandoned, they were immediately made wards of the court and sent to live with the Crain's, who ran a foster home, until Martin was granted custody. Martin panicked as soon as Caroline nailed him to the wall. He tried to console himself that the Crain's were good people, and at least the girls would be safe until he decided what to do. He kept reminding himself that he only intended it to be a temporary solution until he could come up with something better. His girls had already been through so much and he worried how much more they could take. He resented Caroline for putting him in this position but hated himself even more for not being man enough to stand up to her. How dare she?

"I don't know if I'll ever forgive you for this Caroline. You may have pushed me too hard, this time." Martin was weak, however, and they both knew it. As usual, Caroline won this battle too.

***

Foster care was not an easy transition for Edie. She cried for her mother every night. Amy didn't like it either but the Crain's fostered at least half a dozen children most of the time and had a twelve-year-old son of their own so Amy had lots of children to play with. Mr. Crain helped with the children the best he could. He was a sweet man and the children loved him, but he was twenty years older than his wife and slowing down a good bit due to some health problems. All he really could physically do was keep an eye on the children while Diane Crain did all the work which put all the responsibility on her back. They loved him but figured out his limitations right away. The little ones would get him to read to them from his big recliner and then when he dozed off, they would take off and get into whatever they could find. This was frustrating to Diane. She already had a full-time job bathing them, dressing them, feeding them, and seeing the older ones got to school on time, and a hundred other things needed in the care of a child that kept Diane in a constant state of exhaustion. One night, Edie was bathed, in her pajamas and sitting on the side of the tub watching two other small girls still in the tub floating a miniature sailboat. Ms. Crain stepped around the corner to get some extra towels and Bobby Crain, her twelve-year-old son charged in, pushed Edie into the tub, and ran out before his mother even saw him.

"Edie, this isn't like you. Do you think this is funny?" It was all Dianne could do to hold back the tears.

"Ms. Crain, Bobby pushed Edie into the tub," the little girls insisted, both talking at the same time. "She was just sitting on the side of the tub talking to us."

"Girls, I'm sorry. Edie, run into the bedroom and get some dry clothes. Bobby, come here NOW."

Dianne believed them but was furious and tired enough that the girls didn't feel validated, even though she apologized. They were little girls and only knew what they observed; Ms. Crain wasn't her usual sweet self. From their perspective, lately, she was always cross about something.

As exhausted as she was, the fact didn't escape Diane that Edie was the only one of the children who didn't ever tell on Bobby, her renegade son who was always causing problems. She knew from the moment Edie and Amy came to stay with them, there was something special about Edie. On the surface, she eventually adapted well enough but there was a depth to her that the other children didn't share. Even though she sometimes heard Edie crying softly at night in her room she knew this one was a fighter and had strength she herself didn't realize yet. It was Edie's sad eyes that haunted her most of all. Children like Edie were the reason she chose this path. Diane didn't know her story yet but instinctively knew whatever life threw at her, Edie would rise above it. She did have a special relationship with her older sister, Amy and that was definitely in her favor.

"Amy, what's going on?" Diane asked. Edie was on the bed whimpering and Amy was holding and rocking her like a baby on her lap.

"Edie was playing with the other kids, and they were burying each other in the leaves. When she got into bed, she realized a bug had crawled into her ear and I couldn't get it out at first. She was terrified. I told her to lay on her side and I put some Vicks salve in her ear, and it finally fell out. I think it's dead, she said, holding up a Kleenex with the bug in it."

"I'm glad you look out for your little sister, Amy," Diane said, looking at Edie's tear-stained face. "She's fortunate to have you."

God definitely watches out for his little children, though. One morning Edie managed to slip away by herself when everyone was busy, and no one was looking. She thought it would be fun to ride her tricycle down the Crain's driveway. The only problem was their driveway had a steep downward grade to it and the garage door with its glass door panes was down that day. Once Edie was at the top of the driveway and saw the garage door was closed, it was too late to stop. She barely had time to throw her arm up in front of her face, cutting her wrist with the flying glass. Glass shards were lying everywhere.

"Dear God. Edie! What happened?" Dianne asked. Grabbing Edie, she took her to the guest bathroom to the left of the stairs. Don't cry, honey. I'll fix you right up and you'll be fine." The cut to her wrist certainly wasn't life-threatening and should have been stitched. Edie was freaking out from all the blood and Diane had been patching up children for years. Fortunately, it missed a main artery. Diane did a great job stopping the bleeding and bandaging her up. Unfortunately, the little scar it made would be in direct competition to the invisible one she held in her heart trying to understand why she couldn't go home. The next day Dianne took her on the bus for a shopping trip and Edie hated the way people stared at her and kept asking her what happened to her hand. She just wanted to go home and be with her mother.

***

Chapter Five

Edie forced herself to come back to the present, immediately enjoying the beautiful explosion of color all around her as she drove her rental car to Averton Psychiatric Hospital. Spring was her favorite season. It must be a sign. Spring always signified new growth and beginnings to her. Dr. Trent was great about calling regularly with progress updates about her sister but this time he told her Amy had recently made a miraculous breakthrough. To his surprise, after Edie's last visit, Amy gradually started talking and interacting with her environment and others. Edie was so excited she couldn't wait to see her. As she parked her rental car and entered the building, she wondered how long it would be before she could take Amy home. She was so encouraged; she just knew things were going to change for both of them. She told Dr. Trent Amy could stay at her apartment until she got on her feet. They would be able to get reacquainted again after all these years.

The Baby

"Edie, I was just thinking about you," Dr. Trent said. "How are you? Come with me. Your sister is waiting for you."

Edie couldn't believe the change in Amy. She was sitting up straight in a blue velvet tufted armchair and greeted her sister with a warm smile and bright and clear eyes. She wore a stunning blouse of a light pink silky material and a maxi skirt in a floral pattern. She'd fixed her hair, and it fanned around her face in flattering waves.

"Hi Edie," she said, jumping up to give her sister a warm hug. When she hugged Amy back, Edie noticed immediately there was a suspicious bulge on her abdomen.

"Amy, you look amazing," The change in her demeanor was miraculous. "You're glowing. If you don't mind, I'm going to step out and talk to Dr. Trent for a minute. I'll be right back."

"I can't get over the change in Amy, Dr. Trent. What happened? I couldn't help but notice how alert and happy she was. I noticed something else, however, when I hugged her. Is Amy pregnant?"

"Yes, she is, unfortunately, but it's complicated."

"Of course, it's complicated. A couple of months ago she couldn't even complete a sentence and now she's pregnant. How is she ever going to get through this? It could throw her right back where she was or worse. She is carrying the child of a rapist, isn't she? Dear God!"

"Edie, take a deep breath, there is more than just the obvious to be considered here. Unquestionably, your sister has taken a miraculous leap in her progress by reconnecting with you. I didn't want to go into it over the phone, but I think deciding to keep the baby has also played a major role in her dramatic change in behavior as well."

"Keep it? What could she be thinking? I don't understand."

"The baby; she talks of nothing else. Initially, she said she would carry it and give it up for adoption, but it became obvious from the beginning she fell in love with the idea of having someone who would love her back as she put it. It's as if having a child to love has been something she's wanted her whole life. This baby may be the exact catalyst that has given her the desire to live again. If you remember, I told you it wasn't permanent, Edie. Your sister has a strong desire to get well. It could take years of therapy to peel back the layers, but Amy has found a purpose; the oldest one in the book, the love for a child."

"I get what you're saying, but I'm still concerned. She's eventually coming back to live with me anyway and I will help all I can. I hate to state the obvious, but how will she cope with what's happened to her?" Won't the child remind her of the rape every time she looks at it?"

"Your sister has never seen it that way, believe it or not. She sees what happened to her and the baby unconnected in any way."

"The fact is that she had the breakdown in the first place. Is it because our mother was mentally ill our whole lives? Is it hereditary?"

"Not at all. Your sister isn't the only one who suffered in her childhood home in that unhealthy and toxic environment. She chose to put her experiences in a box. The only problem is that strategy rarely works and often compromises healing as well as confuses and distances those around you. One day you will have to choose to face those demons as well."

"I appreciate your concern Dr. Trent, but I already lived that life once. I have no intention of living it again by dredging up old ghosts. Our parents should never have had children. I realize now my mother was mentally ill, possibly even manic-depressive. She was so toxic; I wonder if Amy and I will ever be able to put it behind us. I spent so many years of my life trying to measure up to her crazy standards or whatever they were. I would have stood on my head if I thought it would have made her happy. Of course, it was impossible because she kept changing the rules. I didn't even realize how furious I was with her until I struck out on my own."

"I wondered for years if following through with my singing was my dream or a form of rebellion against my mother. She always told me I better get married and have babies because I wasn't "college material." I heard most of my life I was *slower* than most kids growing up. She told me I didn't walk or talk until I was two. When my dad told me that was insane, it was too late to make a difference. It didn't matter that I had good grades all through school and somehow managed to stay on the honor roll. When I was in high school, Amy was already missing but I wasn't allowed to turn on a radio, television, or operate any kind of machinery in the house for as long as I can remember. One day my mother went into the hospital for throat surgery. I had never turned on the washer or dryer and I was terrified I would break something. The paradox was I did most of the cooking for the last two years I was home. That was different, I guess. She hated to cook so it became my job. The reality was Amy and I never questioned what we were told. Why would we? She was our mother. She seemed to have a propensity for picking men in the military so we stayed on the move; it was a real challenge for us to keep up with that kind of pace. Her husbands were always a lot younger. I guess she thought they would help her stay young forever. She finally settled down with Edwin, our stepfather, but that's another whole story. I think she believed some of the garbage she filled our heads with. To this day, I think I still struggle with not measuring up even though I know now she was mentally ill. One of her especially screwy mantras was, 'Education and a pretty face aren't any good if you don't know how to use them to get what you want.' We couldn't acquire any kind of self-confidence since she was always putting us down and talking about herself and all her successes. I realize now it was how she elevated her shaky ego. She never kept any friends for long. The only time we were around other people was at school or church if Amy took me. Mother didn't drive so we didn't go a lot especially if my stepfather was away on a tour of duty. Then cabs or buses were our usual way of getting around. When Amy was twelve, we were allowed to take a bus downtown and see a movie on the weekend sometimes. When I was allowed to date, I felt like I was let out of a cage."

"Did you and Amy spend a lot of time in church when you were growing up?"

"Not at all. I was ten before I ever stepped foot in a church. We were in Germany at the time and Amy took me to a protestant church on post. The only other choice there was a Catholic church."

"Why didn't your parents take you to church?"

"You know it was never discussed, but I just knew on some level something traumatic must have happened to my mother because she came from a God-fearing family. My stepfather used to boast he was an agnostic. Only once do I remember going to church with Mother in Minneapolis when I was in high school, just the two of us. It was obvious to me she didn't enjoy it. I have no idea why, but I do remember always praying if something went wrong or frightened me when I was small. I guess I picked it up from my friends because I don't remember a time when I didn't believe in God. I'm not sure if Amy kept her faith over the years but she certainly was the one responsible for giving me the exposure."

"So how did it make you feel when she told you, you would never be "college material?"

"How do you think it made me feel? It didn't matter to me that she was crazy. I was a child; I wasn't equipped to process anything so seriously. I was furious with her and heartbroken most of the time. I couldn't get it through my head that she was incapable of giving or receiving love. She definitely wasn't a hugger. I think both Amy and I were starved for affection but didn't know it then. Things were a lot harder for Amy. She hated school and was miserable and homesick when we were overseas, and she had to attend a high school on base fifty miles away. She only came home by train from Munich on the weekends when we were in Germany. One weekend she came home, Mother was out taking a night class, and Edwin, our stepfather snuck into her room and attempted to rape her. Skippy, our dog was trying to get back into the bedroom and started barking and scratching on the door. The coward immediately bolted. Skippy saved Amy from a horrible trauma. She was still traumatized, however, by the whole terrible ordeal and told Mother, but she didn't believe her or said she didn't. Of course, it was never brought up or talked about again. Amy got back on the train for school the upcoming Sunday and she and a friend ran away and stayed in a hotel for two days and then called when they ran out of money. Amy told me she made some surface cuts on her wrists to scare Mother, but it backfired, and Mother signed her into a sanitarium. As young as I was, I believe Mother did it for spite more than anything. Amy never forgave Mother for not believing her or sending her away. What about Amy? You confirmed she is pregnant. Dear God, it's from the rape, isn't it? What's she going to do?"

"Your sister is an amazing woman, Edie, and a survivor. I think she will survive this very well. I'm sure she will tell you how she feels as soon as you girls are together again."

***

Chapter Six

Edie was at Averton for a last visit a few months after Amy was discharged with Dr. Trent and ran into Aaron Weissman in the hall outside the cafeteria.

A strangely familiar man gently touched her arm as she walked by. It startled her. She visibly jumped.

"Edie Carrington, how is your sister? I'm sorry. You must think I'm nuts. I'm Aaron Weissman by the way. I didn't mean to startle you. I recognized your voice from the park the day we met. That was a difficult day for me, I'm afraid. Your picture on your record albums doesn't do you justice." He couldn't believe how beautiful she was. He was hanging out in the day room one day and heard some of the patients saying she was a famous singer. He soon purchased all her albums he could find and listened to them whenever he got the chance. "Would you let me make it up to you for startling you and buy you a cup of coffee? I know I could use some myself."

"You know, you talked me into it. I have some time to kill, and I was on my way to do just that." She realized she didn't recognize him at first because he was blind the last time she saw him, and he carried himself differently. She noticed how attractive he was the first time she saw him on the hospital grounds, but he was surrounded by an aura of sadness like a second skin. It haunted her and she had never forgotten him or his terrible sadness. Now it was impossible to ignore his energy. It was electric and his once blank blue eyes were staring at her once again; only this time it was completely different. This time the effect was making her lightheaded. She remembered she did see him in the hall a couple of times with his service dog. Once he dropped a small transistor radio and she stopped to pick it up for him. His service dog was having some trouble getting a grip on it. They spoke briefly and she commented on his beautiful companion. She was reticent to pet him because she'd heard service dog owners did not want people to interact with them as it might distract them from their responsibilities. Aaron recognized her immediately by her perfume and her voice that day and was surprised at how sad he was when she walked away.

They found a table in the cafeteria by a window overlooking the grounds. Edie wondered if the location he chose was a coincidence or if Aaron was enjoying the view now as well as a whole new world because he had his sight back. She was too polite to ask how he regained his sight even though she was delighted for him. Aaron rushed off to get their coffee.

"I hope you like apple pie," Aaron said. "I have a sweet tooth and didn't want to be rude." He proceeded to remove the two plates of apple pie ala mode and two coffees from the tray and place them on the table.

"Apple pie is one of my favorites, especially with a scoop of ice cream on it."

"How about that? It is a favorite of mine as well. I can tell you I have a serious crush on the cook here. The food isn't too bad for a cafeteria, but the pies are to die for. Do you live in Atlanta, or are you on tour visiting your sister?"

Edie wasn't sure about all the questions but the chemistry between them was undeniable, and at the same time she felt so comfortable with him that it was as if they'd known each other for years.

"No, I don't live here, and I am just getting off on a tour here with my sister Amy. I do have an apartment here in Averton, but I won't be needing it anymore. Dr. Trent has completely released Amy, so it is a great day for both of us. This will be her last visit."

"You're kidding, Dr. Trent is my doctor too. I am just checking in with him for a last visit as well. How is that for a coincidence?"

"That is amazing. Where's that beautiful dog of yours today?"

"Oh, I didn't bring him with me today; he's home pouting, I'm sure. Beacon is my service dog, and we are rarely apart. I have some issues from 'Nam; I was blind the last time you saw me but obviously, that's behind me now. I needed to make a quick trip here and pick up some paperwork. Dr. Trent is an excellent doctor. He has helped me through a lot. I'm glad to hear your sister is doing so well."

"Thank you." Edie was still curious about his story and how he regained his sight, but she didn't want to make him uncomfortable or pry. They talked as if they were old friends until she noticed her watch and couldn't believe two hours had passed already. He caught her off guard when he asked her for her phone number. She was shocked at how fast she was willing to give Aaron her phone number as if she was just waiting for the opportunity. They made an instant connection on the spot. It wasn't just the chemistry. He called the next week and asked her to the movies; they went to dinner afterward and talked for hours. Dating Aaron evolved so naturally that before Edie knew it six months had passed, and it was hard to imagine what her life was like before Aaron was in it. Her career continued to thrive; she was so busy on tour that she barely had time to think about it but when she did, it baffled her. Being able to sing for a living was the realization of a lifelong dream. Aaron was always in the wings supporting her and she knew he was waiting for her at the end of every tour. She did visit Oklahoma City on tour sometimes but seeing each other as often as they wanted was a real challenge for both of them. It was a long-distance romance and a problem for them as he was from Norman, Oklahoma and when she wasn't on tour or staying in hotels, she had an apartment in Averton, where they first met. Averton was a rural town north of Atlanta, Georgia, with a population of barely 150,000. She'd intended to get rid of her apartment when Amy got better and left Averton Hospital but changed her mind. It was convenient to the airport, and she loved being so close to Atlanta anyway.

Life continued on for both Carrington girls at a comfortable pace once Amy left Averton. Amy's due date was getting closer. Of course, life seemed to enjoy throwing them a roadblock here and there, specifically designed for each of them. In spite of her pregnancy, Amy had accomplished so much in a short time. She stayed with Edie for a while as they planned, and she worked on completing her teaching degree and sending out resumes. It was therapeutic for both of them. Neither of them was comfortable enough to delve into their past and stayed crazy busy shaping their futures so it was never discussed. Soon, Amy was ready to spread her wings and found a nice place of her own across town and Edie was off tour for a week and offered to help her move.

"Amy, are you insane? You can't pick up on those boxes." Amy's delivery date was getting close, and she was at that miserable stage. "Let me do that, okay?"

"I'm not going to argue with you, Sis. I don't want anything to happen to my baby."

"Do you still think it's a girl?"

"I do, I have felt from the beginning, I was carrying a little girl."

"That's good enough for me. Promise me you will leave the rest of this mess until I get home. You are welcome to come with me, you know."

"Edie, I appreciate the invitation but I'm afraid you'll have to visit Mother on your own."

"Are you sure? Mother's health is declining at an alarming rate."

"I'm definitely not happy to hear that but I am not willing to subject myself to that kind of pain ever again. I really appreciate all your help here. I thought we'd never get all this stuff packed up."

"You're so welcome. What are sisters for? I'll catch up with you later for dinner after I get back, okay? Don't you dare pick up any of this stuff. If it's in your way I can move it when I get back. Maybe we can go to Bentleys and be waited on in the style we deserve."

Edie was pulling into her mother's driveway with mixed feelings. She was deep in thought and barely aware of the immaculate and elaborate landscaping that graced her mother's generous lot. What was she even doing here? Amy was right; her mother would never change. If she had any sense, she would follow her example and avoid their mother like the plague.

"Edie, I'm so glad you made it. I have coffee and scones. Sit down, dear, there in front of me. That is one of my more comfortable chairs."

In her prime, Octavia Carrington Martin had been a breathtaking beauty, but many years of rheumatoid arthritis had ravaged her body and taken its toll. Over the years, her posture had become severely compromised and her spine was in a permanent hunched-over position. As a result, it was a challenge for her to look up at someone if she was standing as the pain and stiffness barely allowed her to lift her head. Her housekeeper brought in a tray and sat it down on the coffee table between them. As Octavia filled Edie's cup with coffee from the elegant carafe, Edie was shocked at how twisted and shaky her mother's hands were and suspected she must be in a great deal of pain. As she leaned forward and handed Edie a cup of steaming coffee with a linen napkin, she picked up the plate of scones and passed it to her with shaky hands. Edie took one and set the plate of remaining scones on the massive, beveled glass coffee table in front of them.

"My poor beautiful Edie, you look tired. Are you getting enough sleep dear?"

"Yes, Mother, and I'm not tired. I've been helping Amy pack up. She has found a lovely apartment and is moving out this weekend."

"I'm afraid your puffy eyes say otherwise. You'll never catch a man looking like that. I raised you to take better care of yourself, you know. You've come a long way from that ugly little baby they brought to me in the hospital. I thought they had switched babies on me. The doctor used forceps during the delivery and your eyes were swollen shut. I didn't know what color your eyes were for weeks. You have a responsibility to take care of your looks. Once they're gone, they're gone. I suppose I'll never see Amy again. I can only imagine what trumped-up offense she has concocted against me this time. All those years we didn't know whether she was dead or alive. Surely, she doesn't blame me for that too."

"I don't know, Mother. I'm afraid that's between you and Amy." She wondered what her mother would say if she knew Amy was pregnant with her grandchild. When her

42

mother leaned forward to put her empty cup and saucer on the coffee table, she saw a picture of Edwin behind her on the mantle and shuddered. The man had been dead for years, but her visceral reaction was from a cellular level. "Mother, I've brought you a surprise, a copy of my newest album. It's fresh out of production and won't be on the market for another week. You'll be one of the first people to hear it."

"That's very thoughtful of you dear, but you know classical music is all I listen to. I don't understand the music today. It's so *raucous*. I still can't believe you have chosen a music career over the security of a man with an established career who could financially support you with style."

Edie set the album her mother so obviously rejected and left Edie still holding it in her hand, down on the hideous ornate carved Elizabethan chair her mother never allowed anyone to sit on. "It's been nice, Mother but I have to go."

"Okay, it's obvious you're upset. What did I say this time? I see you haven't changed much. You've always been much too sensitive and have worn your feelings on your sleeve. I believe in telling it the way I see it. I'm sorry if you see it otherwise. Come back when you can stay longer."

Edie gave her mother a quick hug even though she was the least tactual person she knew. Olivia's response was immediate, and she stiffened the moment their bodies made contact. Edie walked quietly to the front door.

Chapter Seven

As soon as the door closed, Olivia Carrington Martin rose stiffly from the couch, struggling with the rheumatic pain that ravaged her body, and walked to the window to watch her daughter hurry down the long walkway to her car until she could no longer see her. She turned from the window, walked slowly into her office, and pulled an album out of a drawer in the massive credenza that sat against one wall. She sat down at her desk and looked at every page of clippings, photos, announcements, and programs she had collected over the entire life of Edie's career. As always, she wondered with regret what made her say and do the things she did. It was as if she was driven to hurt the ones she loved. She knew Edie was special so why did she emotionally abuse her every time she saw her? She was immensely proud of Edie but couldn't bring herself to tell her. She knew Amy, on the other hand, hated her. A pervasive loneliness consumed her as she walked back into the living room and to her beloved Elizabethan chair and picked up the album Edie had left for her. When she straightened up and turned around, she saw the picture of Edwin on her fireplace mantle, cursed him under her breath, and forgot all about the album and her desire to play it. She could pick them, couldn't she?

***

"Edwin, we need to talk. I want a divorce."

"A divorce? Haven't I given you everything you ever wanted? You have a house most people only dream about, cars, expensive clothes, jewelry, vacations abroad, more money than you can ever spend, and you want a divorce? My Uncle Donald would roll over in his grave if he knew of your spending habits and how much of my inheritance you have squandered over the years. You've got to be kidding. I knew you were selfish, but this is ridiculous. Where is your loyalty after all these years? What about my feelings? What if I don't want a divorce?"

"Don't you dare condescend to me. My daughters won't visit me because of you."

"And that's supposed to be my fault. Amy is so full of herself she doesn't have time for you. Who just takes off for twelve years and never lets her family know where she is, anyway? As for Edie, she's always been a carbon copy of you; thinks she is better than everybody else."

"I'm sorry Edwin, I'm already packed, and I'll come back for the rest of my things next week. I should have left years ago. You know this marriage has been dead for years. I'm just putting it to rest.

"Olivia, please, I need you. Please don't leave."

Olivia was unprepared for Edwin's reaction but once she'd made up her mind she couldn't wait to get out. She could never undo the years she'd spent with Edwin and all the emotional fallout they had caused the girls. One day she would burn in Hell for all she'd done but for now, she wanted a fresh start. She heard a loud crash of some sort as

45

she slammed the front door. Too bad, let him throw all her crystal against the door. She was free now. She couldn't care less about a little crystal. She couldn't get her things in the car fast enough. If he continued to act like this, she would just leave the rest of her things behind. She would make sure her lawyer got her a generous alimony. It wasn't like Edwin couldn't afford it.

Olivia was relaxing in a coffee shop, enjoying a latte and a blueberry muffin. Numerous bags sat at her feet. She'd been shopping for herself and enjoying every minute of it. She didn't need to answer to anyone how much she spent anymore and felt giddy with the freedom. She should have done this years ago.

"Excuse me, ma'am, are you Olivia Martin?"

"Yes, I am."

"Your daughter is looking for you. She says it's an emergency."

"An emergency? Wonder what my husband has come up with this time."

"Madam, she says she is your daughter and is calling from the hospital. You are welcome to take the call here." She handed Olivia the phone with the long cord, stepped behind the counter, and began arranging some pastries in the showcase under the counter.

"Hello, Edie has something happened to Amy? Are you okay?"

"No Mother, we're okay. Edwin is at Barrow Memorial Hospital. The doctor says he's had a stroke. He's in a coma right now. Can you come? I can stay until you get here."

"Of course, I'll be there. I'm leaving right now." Wasn't this just like Edwin? He's in for a shock if he thinks I'm the one who's going to take care of him.

When Olivia arrived at Barrow Memorial Hospital, she wasn't prepared to see all the tubes and hospital paraphernalia he was hooked up to.

"Mrs. Martin, I'm Dr. Phenergan. Your husband had a massive stroke and the next twenty-four hours will be crucial, I'm afraid."

"Mother, I'm sorry I need to go. They couldn't get hold of you, so they called me. I'm glad they were able to catch me, but I am supposed to fly out first thing in the morning; I still have to pack."

"Isn't that just hunky-dory? I guess I'll be stuck taking care of Edwin now as if I haven't sacrificed enough already in my life."

Eventually, Edwin did wake up from his coma and when he did Olivia's world changed overnight. He was home from the hospital; he couldn't speak, and the right side of his body was paralyzed. At first, it didn't look as if he knew what planet he was on and she hired nurses around the clock to feed, bathe, and change him. As time went on, he did regain a minimal awareness of some kind. He was right-handed and still had to be fed as his muscles were so weak when he tried with his left hand, food went everywhere, and it enraged him. He still couldn't speak but he could make enough noise, there was little doubt what he wanted as he carried on until he was understood. One foreboding development was a disarming stare that became part of his day, and it was always directed at Olivia. It unnerved her as he would stare at her whenever she walked into the room, and his eyes would follow her until she left the room. If she asked him what he wanted, he would grunt and point a shaky finger at her with his left arm. Olivia had never felt such hatred in her life and was grateful he couldn't say what was on his mind. She resented being back with him but felt some twisted obligation to stay as she knew if she'd never married him, her girls would have had a much different life.

What Olivia couldn't know was Edwin didn't hate her. He was frustrated and, in a panic, because he couldn't communicate, and was consumed with unbearable guilt for the terrible things he had done in his life. As he lay in bed it was all he could think of.

***

Edwin was in his own private Hell long before the doctor said he was unaware of his surroundings. Even though he wasn't in a coma anymore he was experiencing a whole life review of his own. At first, he relived Sundays walking to the little white church in the small town he grew up in Montana with his parents and the wonderful Sunday dinners his mother prepared with so much love. His parents were in love, and he could feel it. Life was good until his mother got sick. At first, he could feel something was different. Meals weren't the same and the house seemed in disarray most of the time. His dad seemed anxious and would fly off the handle at the drop of a hat.

"Edwin, your mother is very ill, son."

"How ill Dad? I know she sleeps a lot, but she says she is tired. Couldn't you hire someone to help her around the house? Tommy's parents have a housekeeper. She cooks too."

"Your mother has cancer, son. A housekeeper isn't going to solve her problems. She needs surgery, but the doctors are afraid it is too advanced, and she might not survive the surgery. The prognosis is grim, I'm afraid."

It seemed as soon as Edwin and his father had that conversation, his world fell apart. He was devastated but his father lacked the fortitude or stamina to hold up under the blow that fate had dealt them. It was as if the closer his mother got to dying, the more his father shrunk into himself. He couldn't eat or sleep. Even though they had a nurse to help, his father hardly left her side. When he did sleep it was on a rollaway bed he put in their room beside their bed. His mother was in so much pain his father was afraid he would disturb her if he slept in their bed. When his mother died his father appeared to be in an upright position, but it was as if he had left his body."

48

"Please, can you send an ambulance right away to 1225 Barone? I don't know what's wrong with my father. He has not left his chair in three days, has soiled himself, and can't speak. I think he's had a stroke." When the ambulance arrived and carried his father away, Edwin was only eleven and had nowhere to go. His father hadn't suffered a stroke but was completely catatonic and his doctors admitted him to a psychiatric hospital.

"I'm sorry son, but you are too young to be on your own. It will hopefully only be for a little while until your dad gets better," Dr. Allen said. "Alcon Home for Boys is one of our best boy's schools. You can request to ride in their van and visit your dad now and then. Work hard and do what you are told, and the time will go quickly." Shortly after he arrived one of his teachers seemed to take an interest in him and Edwin was too innocent to recognize that he was being groomed for a sinister world he could never have imagined. By the time he realized what was happening the assaults became an almost nightly event. He told one of his teachers, but he had such a reputation for being in trouble for so long that no one believed him. The first chance he got, he ran away and wound up on the streets. It was then that he decided if there was a God, he had abandoned him. It wasn't until he was eighteen that he lied about his age and went into the service. At least he didn't have to worry about where his next meal was coming from. He never requested to see his dad when he was at Alcon House and after he went into the service, he never tried to find out what happened to his dad. It was as if that boy died when he ran away and he had blotted out the good memories with the bad. Edwin was too bitter and angry to share his pain with anyone and because of it, his impenetrable shroud of rage became a part of who he was.

I guess am paying for my sins and well deserve it. Edwin thought. "Dear God if you can hear me at all, please forgive me for the life I have led. I can't bear it any longer and I beg of you to take me now." He knew he wasn't making a sound but finally managed to get Olivia's attention and got her to bring him some paper and a pen. He scribbled. "Please forgive me for all I have done."

She couldn't believe what she was reading. A little late, isn't it, Edwin? She thought. How could she forgive him when she couldn't forgive herself? She married him for his money and security. She compromised the welfare of her children for money and blatantly ignored their needs.

It was only days after Edwin scribbled an apology to Olivia on paper begging her forgiveness that he closed his eyes and quietly slipped away. Although Olivia was surprised when she found him the next morning, she was relieved. If only she could go back and relive her life, it could have been so different for her and the girls. The funeral was the required traditional event but small. Edwin was a successful businessman but had been a cruel employer and had made many enemies and few friends. There were only a few people who attended his services other than his family. She was shocked that neither of the girls were there. She thought they could have attended for her sake. It was a sad reflection of his legacy. When his attorney read the will, he left his entire estate to Olivia except for a generous trust for Edie and Amy. Olivia was relieved that she would never have to worry about money again. She had no empathy for him and wondered when she had become so cold. It was a fact that she married Edwin for his money but when did her self-absorption start and who was Olivia and where had she gone? She only hoped God would be able to forgive her for her selfishness and her failure as a parent.

Chapter Eight

Olivia's mind wandered to the days when she was a child, the firstborn and spoiled rotten.

"Daddy, will you buy me that guitar for my lessons?" The minute she saw it in the window, she had to have it.

"I'm sorry honey. We'll have to pick out something a little less expensive."

"But I want that one, Daddy. I don't want another one." she wailed, turning red in the face, and stomping her feet. Of course, she got the guitar she wanted; she always got what she wanted. At six she'd already learned how to manipulate her father. She heard her parents talking one day and knew they were expecting a boy when she was born but that was fine with her. They had her and didn't need a boy. Her dad taught her how to do all kinds of things on the farm and she followed him everywhere. She was his world and his only child. It wasn't until her brother came along that things changed. Her father finally got his boy, and everybody knew it. He told anyone who would listen. and she felt completely ignored.

"Why can't I go with Daddy to the co-op and the pub, Momma, and Peter can?"

"Because you're growing up and young ladies can't hang out at the same places their fathers and sons do. It just isn't appropriate." That was just the beginning. Eventually, she had three brothers. Later, when they got to go to college, she was told she couldn't. "Girls get married and raise families." Her dad said. She never forgave her father even though she did leave home and married right out of high school. There was never enough money for her to go to college in the early years of her marriage. As the years went by and she had two girls to raise, she gave up. She never let their father or her husband forget it either and she carried her rage like a permanent badge and woe to anyone that got in her way.

***

What a mistake it was to expose herself to the usual emotional abuse her mother always seemed to enjoy inflicting on her. It would be a cold day in Hell before she subjected herself to this kind of abuse again. Fighting tears, Edie's hands were shaking when she put her car in reverse and backed out of her mother's driveway. She didn't have long to dwell on her feelings by the time she got home.

"Amy, what's wrong?" Edie could see Amy was in full labor the minute she walked in the door and took one look at her. How far apart are your pains?" It was a week before her due date, but they had an emergency plan in place. Edie hurried to Amy's bedroom, grabbed the little suitcase, took her by the arm, and helped her to the door. They took the elevator to the ground floor of her apartment building and Edie helped her into the car.

"Edie, do you have to hit every pothole in Atlanta? Slow down, I don't want to have her in the car." When they arrived at the hospital's emergency entrance, Amy was whisked away, and Edie was still pacing back and forth when a nurse came out and told her she was an aunt to a beautiful little girl not even an hour later. She went to the nursery and couldn't believe how beautiful the baby was. She was so proud of Amy. This little girl was going to have all the love Amy had been saving all her life to give.

"Amy, she is beautiful. Have you decided on a name yet? I can't believe you knew you were carrying a little girl."

"I have; Amanda Elaine Carrington, after our grandmother."

"Oh, I love that," she said, leaning over and kissing Amy on the cheek. "I am so proud of you. I can't wait until it's time for her to come home. There's no way you can move into your apartment now. You'll have to stay with me for a few weeks. I'll help you. I'll just call Travis and change my tour dates. I was going to be off in another week anyway. He'll be fine with it. Change keeps him young."

It was a wonderful time for the two sisters. Even though Amanda was born a week early, her doctor let her, and the baby go home when he learned Amy would have round-the-clock help.

"Amy, go back to bed. I can handle this," she said as they practically ran into each other in the kitchen. "It's my turn to take care of you for a change. Tomorrow, you can help me if you like, and we'll get more bottles ready. Tonight, you need to rest. Amanda will get her days and nights right in a few weeks, I'm sure." She couldn't help but notice the relief on Amy's face and her heart soared as Amy padded back to her bedroom. She silently said a prayer thanking God for reuniting them and giving her a beautiful baby niece to love.

The days flew by but neither of the two girls would ever forget how special their time was together. Life may have separated them for twelve years, but they were now grown women and it was as if they had never been apart and a whole new phase of their life was unfolding.

***

One night, Aaron and Edie were walking from the Starling Theatre to Aaron's car and Edie said she needed to make a quick trip back to the restroom. When Amy got back Aaron was facing the passenger side of his beloved Pontiac Grand Am and smoking a cigarette with his back to her. She ran up to him, wrapped her arms around his waist, and gave him a big bear hug. In an instant he jumped, whirled around, the cigarette flew from his fingers, and he grabbed her with a death grip by her shoulders. His eyes were those of a madman ready for the kill. He let her go immediately when she called out his name, but Edie was stunned and struggled to understand what had just happened. She could still feel the pressure from his fingers, and he grabbed her by the shoulders.

"Oh, dear God, Edie, I'm so sorry. Let's get in the car for a minute, please. Hear me out, I need to explain my irrational behavior." He opened the passenger door for Edie to get in. Edie got into the car like a robot. She was in shock over Aaron's behavior and devastated. She did notice he was shaking like a leaf when he put his hand on her back as she slid into the car and sat down. Something was wrong.

"Edie, I don't know where to start. It's difficult to explain the life of combat to a civilian. In combat training, we are programmed to be "trained killing machines." We don't consciously think to kill. It is a trained reaction and when someone comes up behind you with a knife or any weapon and grabs you, they have only one objective, kill you. One night, the VC broke into our camp in 'Nam. A guerilla fighter came up behind me, grabbed me, pulled my head back with one hand, and put a knife to my throat with the other."

"Dear God, what happened?"

"I had a bigger knife, fortunately, for me but not so fortunate for him. It was either him or me. That's the life of combat. It could have just as easily been me. War programs us to do things we wouldn't think of doing in real life. I am so sorry. Please don't ever come up behind me like that again. I'm not sure if I'd be able to catch myself before I reacted on autopilot. Do you think I'm nuts?"

"Don't worry, I won't. No, I don't think you're crazy, but I have to admit, I can't begin to wrap my mind around what you've been through or the damage it has done. Give me some time, and work with me, okay? At the same time, it's hard to understand you don't trust me enough to talk about these things. In the meantime, I think we need to make an appointment for you to see a professional."

"I'll do anything for you Edie. I am not sure about a head shrinker; even though, I suppose it wouldn't hurt. Don't forget, I was seeing Dr. Trent when we met."

"I remember, but this is different than your "hysterical blindness" even if it's all related." It's as if you're reliving the war sometimes but your reality is distorted or skewed, and you are having trouble transitioning back and forth."

The Perfect Job

"Ms. Carrington, how are you?" Mr. Elliot asked, extending his hand. "I'm the principal here. I've been going over your resume. Your credentials are certainly impressive, and I think you might be the person we're looking for. You're quite the scholar, aren't you? You wouldn't be related to Edie Carrington in some way, would you? Please sit down and tell me how you heard about us. I noticed you indicated on your application that you have a young child of your own. Does Mr. Carrington share your interest in academia?"

"Yes, as a matter of fact, we are related. Edie is my sister. My husband is not in the picture right now."

"Oh, my goodness," he said, avoiding the obvious unanswered question. Whatever her story was, he was comfortable that it was none of his business. "I wasn't expecting that. I love her music. I have every one of her albums. Tell me, what brings you here to Emerson High School?"

Brent Elliot carried his title well. He loved children and it was reciprocal. He was like the pied piper of children. At forty-six, with the first signs of greying and the beginning of a middle-aged belly, Brent Elliot wasn't a handsome man. One never noticed because he always had a big smile for everyone, and people automatically felt relaxed and comfortable around him. He was a tall man, 6'4" and lanky. He had a permanent limp he'd acquired from falling out of a deer stand when his leg was impaled by a large branch that caused permanent muscle damage. Some might call him a "man's man," but that wouldn't be true. He adored women but was terrified of them; broke out in a sweat whenever he tried to talk to one. He never let that stop him though and kept trying, never giving up hope there was a special person out there waiting for him somewhere.

"I'm not originally from Atlanta but I love children and have been doing some research. I discovered Emerson High has a stellar reputation and that immediately appealed to me. I would love to be part of a school that makes that extra effort to accommodate its students. I'll come right to the point, Mr. Elliot, my credentials may be impressive, but they are pretty recent. I spent a year in a psychiatric hospital because I had a complete breakdown. I'm fine now. I hope that won't be a deterrent or keep me from getting the job. I can give you my doctor's number and he can validate what I've just told you."

"That won't be necessary. I have to commend you on your absolute honesty. It takes a lot of courage to be so truthful and I appreciate it. Honesty just happens to be especially important to me and I believe vital in our world here. You have my word that your personnel file will be privacy-protected with the same integrity that all of our employees are entitled to. Welcome aboard, Ms. Carrington, you'll be teaching history and biology in room 205. You can start first thing next week. Come, I'll show you to your room and introduce you to some of your coworkers."

"Thank you so much, Mr. Elliot. You won't be disappointed."

Chapter Nine

Amy couldn't believe her good luck. Her first week at Emerson High was tedious enough but she fell in love with her students and had never been afraid of hard work. The week flew by, and she couldn't wait to get back. Mr. Elliot was so supportive, and she could see why the staff and students liked him so much. People just naturally wanted to please him, and she was no exception. She was grateful he had taken a chance on her, and she wouldn't disappoint him. She felt a real sense of pride in herself, and it had been a long time since she'd felt that way. It was like she had awakened from a deep sleep. She couldn't wait to share her good luck with Edie.

Edie was thrilled that Amy had survived her breakdown, gone back to school, got her teaching degree, and landed a dream job teaching history and biology in a high school close to her apartment. She deserved every bit of it. Additionally, she was raising a small child on her own. She couldn't be prouder of her sister. Everything was perfect in Edie's world, except for her private struggle with depression and self-esteem issues at times. She'd always been a pro at hiding her problems from the world. Her very career depended on it. That is until she met and fell in love with Aaron. It was like he could look into her soul at times.

"Edie honey, what's going on? I can feel your sadness," Aaron said as he held her in the hot tub on the patio of her apartment. "It's like a dark cloud hanging over you." She was leaning up against his chest so she couldn't see his handsome face. He didn't need to see her face to know tears were silently running down her cheeks. The water was hot, but he could detect a slight shiver now and then as she desperately tried to reel in her emotions.

"I don't know. It's crazy! I have everything I ever dreamed of. My career is flourishing. I have you, the most important person in my life. Even Amy seems well, standing on her own two feet, has landed a dream job, and is doing a fine job raising Amanda on her own, so what is my problem? I feel so empty and numb sometimes. I love you and I know you love me. Why isn't that enough? Is it because sometimes I just can't let go of my old tapes about not being good enough? When will enough ever be enough?"

"Come here, honey," he said, pulling her down on his lap. She was vaguely aware of the pleasant aromatic lavender fragrance emanating from the Jacuzzi's bath oils.

"You know when I got back from 'Nam, I felt dead inside. In a way, it began to feel natural and when I started to work through it, it was terrifying. All I wanted to do then was to revert to my safe and numb cocoon. Thanks to you, I believe now getting professional help is the healthiest thing I can do for myself. As frightening as it is, I know it's the only way I can have a normal life. The journey may be a trip into the same Hell I came out of, but the message is the same." Getting out of the Jacuzzi, he grabbed a luxurious terry cloth robe from a nearby chair and helped her out of the Jacuzzi into his waiting arms. "Edie, you, and Amy were given horrible messages growing up. Ironically, your mother always told you she should never have had you because she was right. She was too toxic to ever have children. Unfortunately, when our ego is continuously attacked, one way to survive is to blunt our emotions. We might function brilliantly in our everyday world but can't feel the joy life has to offer. Think of the butterfly. A monarch butterfly lives for up to nine months, and that's only the last generation of each year. The average species' lifespan is only two weeks, the male slightly less. Think of how precious life is to them. We only have one time around and need to make the most of it in the short time we are here. All your life you've pursued and actualized your dream. Your fans have fallen in love with you. What you don't realize yet is you already have the love you've sought all these years but until you can look within and fall in love with yourself, you will always feel empty. It requires finding out who you are and completely revamping your self-image."

"I can't believe you're real, Aaron. Where have you been hiding all my life?"

"I don't know, but I never believed in soul mates until I met you. If you could see what I see you'd know. We'll heal each other. We can be like the butterflies and live every precious moment with everything we have because we are here for such a short time."

Aaron decided to move to Averton into a small apartment to be closer to Edie and it was making things a lot easier for both of them. He was able to go back to school under his

GI bill and pick up the hours he needed to become a flight instructor. It wasn't OU but he was able to transfer most of his credits to the university successfully. Suddenly, it was imminently clear a medical career was what his parents wanted, not him. They were gone now, he missed them terribly, but he realized with a shock, that he didn't have to worry about disappointing them anymore. He was shocked when he found out how well off financially his parents were. He knew they took wonderful vacations every year and he'd never wanted for anything as a child. At the same time, his dad emphasized a strong work ethic and always had a plan for the future. When Aaron discovered girls, he never thought about it much or his future in his wilder days. He was having too much fun and flying by the seat of his pants was his approach to life. Those days seemed so far behind him now.

"Aaron, you are a very wealthy young man." Mr. McCray, his dad's lawyer said.

"I beg your pardon. I know my dad considered himself somewhat of an expert in investing, but my parents both worked my whole life growing up."

"That's true but your dad was an expert in investing and saving among other things. His estate is worth over two and a half million not counting his stocks and investments and the beach house in Cape Cod. Since you're an only child, you are the sole heir. You'll never have to work another day in your life if you don't want to."

"Wait a minute, I thought the beach house belonged to Stan, my uncle."

"Seriously, you mean the drunk. When was the last time you saw your uncle?"

"I barely remember what he looks like; years I guess."

"Exactly, and your dad had a good reason for that. Your Uncle Stan is an alcoholic; was always hitting your dad up for money. He has been homeless for years; your dad has made a modest concession for him in his will with explicit instructions for you, so he can't squander it away on alcohol. We'll meet again soon and go over everything. In the meantime, congratulations."

Aaron was in shock and couldn't understand why his dad never told him how well off he was. Did his mom know? He was amazed she never told him. He had no idea, but he was going to do exactly what he always planned. Now he could pursue his dreams and not worry about money. Aaron continued to spend time training on base and keeping his flight hours up enough on the weekends to maintain his flight status. Flying was in his blood, and it would always be. He missed being in the air so much, but he wasn't comfortable putting his wings back on until he could get his head on straight. Until then he would just have to be content with the flight simulator; Thanks to Edwin Link for his invention and patent for its first use in 1929. He knew he needed help and if Edie wanted him to see another shrink, he would no matter how much it freaked him out. A promise was a promise. He was surprised at how much he loved being an instructor. The pay wasn't terrific, but he could choose his hours and work part-time on the base and still finish school. Now he wouldn't have to worry about that anymore. He couldn't imagine doing anything else.

***

"Where are we going Aaron, I'm starved. Why are you being so mysterious?"

"Can't I surprise my girl once in a while? If I tell you, it won't be a surprise, will it? I forgot something, honey, I need to go by my place, okay? Come on, it's too cold for you to sit in the car."

"Aaron, what have you done? This is beautiful. When did you have time to do all this? I love it."

As soon as Edie followed Aaron into his apartment, she saw the dining room table was set for two, complete with candles, a linen tablecloth, napkins, and all. A beautiful vase of long-stemmed red and white roses sat in the center of the table.

"Come sit down," Aaron said as he pulled out a chair for her. Beacon beamed with pride and an expression that made her wonder later if the closeness he shared with Aaron enabled him to sense the importance of the evening. It was as if he reflected whatever Aaron felt.

The food was delicious. Aaron chose to serve a salmon souffle, asparagus, wild rice, and a light salad. By the time he served dessert, Edie was stuffed but picked up her spoon so she wouldn't hurt Aaron's feelings. It was a mouthwatering bread pudding with rum sauce and whipped cream, so Edie was completely taken by surprise when her spoon made a strange sound on something like metal. "Oh, dear." She looked at Aaron and he looked like the proverbial cat that swallowed the canary. Grabbing her hand and taking the ring from her fingers, he carefully wiped it off with a damp napkin he'd dipped into a water glass, got down on one knee, and said. "Edie, you are my everything. I can't imagine ever living another day without you. Not only do I love you, but you are my best friend. You are so beautiful. I love the crazy way you twirl your hair around your finger when you're concentrating. I fell in love with your voice the first time I heard it at Averton before I ever met you or saw what you looked like. Will you marry me?"

"I thought you'd never ask. Yes. Yes. Yes."

"Me either." He laughed, slipping the glittering three-carat Solitaire diamond engagement ring on her finger. Edie would have to find out later how he knew her size because it fit as if it were made for her. It was so elegant it took her breath away. He got up, leaned over, gave her a deep and passionate kiss, picked her up tenderly, and carried her to the bedroom.

Chapter Ten

Their wedding was like a dream. It was everything Edie could have ever imagined and more. She took some much-needed time off between tours. It was a small but beautiful wedding. Her mother was the only one of their parents left and true to character, chose not to attend, but most of their friends were there. Amy looked radiant and beautiful as her maid of honor. They decided to get married on the beautiful grounds by the pond at Averton where they first met. Even Dr. Trent surprised everyone by being there. Aaron had spared no expenses. Edie's gown was spectacular, a sleeveless V-neck beaded floor-length white satin ball-length gown with hand-applied lace roses on the skirt. Her dark curls were pulled up with the baby's breath woven through. Aaron's eyes teared up when he saw her. She was so beautiful he realized he was holding his breath when he

65

saw Travis Perrin, her manager and mentor walk towards him with Edie on his arm. The weather was perfect. It was an especially romantic environment, as they took their vows in front of the beautiful gazebo adorned with pink and white miniature roses. There was a path of rose petals from the bench that Aaron was sitting on when they met leading to the gazebo. Of course, Beacon was there with his majestic stature and intelligent eyes. Aaron had even adorned him with a black and white polka-dotted bow tie commiserate for the occasion. The weather was made to order and afterward, guests walked past the pond and across the grounds to a modest-sized indoor ballroom to enjoy the band. Edie surprised Aaron by singing their favorite song, *We've Only Just Begun*. They danced the night away into the wee hours of the morning with their guests.

Aaron took off some time from his teaching at the airfield and school as well and surprised Amy with a two-week-long honeymoon in romantic Paris. She was shocked that people recognized her that far away for her music. Aaron beamed. The food was delicious. They discovered the romantic and renowned Le Fouquet's.

"Aaron, this is the most delicious chocolate I have ever put in my mouth."

"I agree. It should come with a warning; not responsible if you have to buy different clothes before you go home."

Fouquet's, the legendary mouthwatering confectionary shop with its pink lighting, which gave it a dreamy warm glow, was on the ground floor. A wonderful black iron spiral staircase led upstairs to a romantic restaurant where guests could look outside and watch people walking by on the ground level if they were fortunate enough to have reserved a table by a window. Aaron had reserved a table by a window ahead of time and Edie would never forget dining with the coveted view of beautiful "La Ville Lumiere," The City of Lights before them. Of course, the wines were exquisite. They soaked up everything they could, the Arc de Triomphe, the Cathedral Notre Dame, and the Louvre Museum. She was a little disappointed that the *Mona Lisa* was so small. She learned the renowned Leonardo da Vinci painting had been encased in glass since the 1950's after a visitor poured acid at it. There just wasn't enough time to see everything and they promised each other they would come back for many anniversaries. On their last night in Paris, they dined at a restaurant close to the Eiffel Tower and walked outside at midnight in time to see the glittering lights of the tower that sparkle for five minutes at the hour. She would never forget it. The ten-hour flight back home seemed to go by faster than before as they slept a good bit and chattered about getting home and starting their new life together. They decided they would let go of Aaron's place when they got home and live at Edie's apartment until they decided at some point to buy their dream home. Beacon would be so glad to see them, and Edie would have a week-long tour in three states soon after they got back.

"Beacon, there you are!" Aaron grabbed him and struggled to keep his balance as Beacon leaped into his arms. "You missed me, didn't you boy?" It took a while for Beacon to settle down but finally, he lay down in front of the fireplace looking on top of the world. "Whoa, where are you going beautiful?" Grabbing Edie, as she walked past him, he gave her a long and slow kiss. "You still make my toes curl every time we kiss. I love you so much, Edie. What do you say we put Beacon out, and retire to the Jacuzzi, Mrs. Weissman?"

Hearing the conversation, Beacon made a beeline to the pantry and sat down with one paw up waiting for a treat. If they were going to put him out, he might as well use his body language to his advantage and assume his best guilt position before he got his walking papers. His saddest face didn't work as well as he hoped, however, since Aaron put him out anyway and without a treat. All was soon forgiven when he immediately saw a squirrel looking at him and just waiting to be chased up the closest tree. After they got out of the Jacuzzi, wrapped only in their towels, they made love like it was their first time, falling asleep in each other's arms.

***

Not even a month after their dream honeymoon, one morning Aaron woke up and decided to get up and make some coffee. Edie was still asleep. He felt a little shaky as if he had been startled or was suffering from a sugar crash. It was way too early for food. Vaguely, he remembered he had a nightmare the night before but couldn't retrieve the details. He grabbed a clean pair of briefs and a T-shirt from the dresser and headed down the hall for the kitchen trying not to wake up Edie. He was barely aware of preparing the coffee pot. As it started to drip, he began reminiscing about their honeymoon. All of a sudden, he was mentally yanked back into 'Nam, his heart pounding, right in the middle of an ambush. They had successfully succeeded in removing Charlie from the perimeter; dead bodies were everywhere. He was apprehensive about a piece of a building a few yards ahead of him. It was only a dilapidated shell from all the fallout, but he was afraid Charlie could be hiding inside. Charlie was a formidable and dangerous opponent; they were the invaders of a foreign land. It was Charlie's terrain after all, and they knew every inch of it like the back of their hand. Nothing could be taken for granted. If you had a feeling, you better check it out. Satisfied it was all clear inside and alerting his men behind him; he took off his helmet for a minute to wipe the sweat and dirt from his eyes. Immediately he felt something dripping on his head. Wiping his wet face, he realized it was blood coming from a hole in the ceiling. Running outside he saw one of his men lying on his back on the flimsy metal roof bleeding out; his body bullet-ridden and ravaged from a bayonet.

The next thing he knew, he woke up and was in the hospital with absolutely no memory of how he got there. The last thing he remembered was in the kitchen making coffee. The nightmares were back and now he was having flashbacks. How in the hell did he get to this point and couldn't remember what happened in between? He couldn't imagine what Edie must be going through. They only kept him in the hospital for three days providing he agreed to see the psychiatrist they referred him to as soon as he got home.

Aaron was furious. He was married to his soul mate and suddenly the demons were back invading his life again. It was totally unacceptable. He knew they were always in the background waiting to pounce on him, but why now? It was 1974 and he had been back from that hellhole for three years now and started waking up in the middle of the night again screaming, soaking wet with sweat. He dreamt about unknown faces, faces he didn't recognize but he knew somehow, they were the faces of the dead he and he alone had killed. Until he woke up in the hospital, he stopped having that recurring nighttime horror that propelled him out of a deep sleep screaming. It was the first time since they were married. It freaked Edie out and he was devastated the nightmares were back. He was a fool to think just because they were so happy, they would let him have any peace.

One prior nightmare that threatened to derail him was always the same. Just as his helicopter would get close enough to the LZ, (landing zone) he would see this young Vietnamese girl shoot an RPG (rocket-propelled grenade) at them but miss and she would mouth the words, "You deserve this, Meo Huang," just before she imploded from the mortar rounds his gunner dropped from the helicopter.

***

69

Chapter Eleven

"Mr. Weissman, you may come in. Dr. Faraday will see you now."

"Well, hello! And who is this handsome fellow?" Dr. Faraday asked. Squatting down on one knee, he put his hand out and the magnificent golden retriever politely offered his golden paw in return.

"Mr. Weissman, it is my extreme pleasure to meet you. Please take a seat with your copilot here."

"Beacon, his name is Beacon."

"All right, then, Aaron and Beacon, please have a seat." Beacon immediately lay down at Aaron's feet and put his head gently down on his paws as if to sleep but sleep was the last thing on his mind. He was on sentry duty; it was what he was trained to do.

"Aaron, what brought you here today to see me?"

"My wife called the little men in white jackets on me, and my butt landed in the hospital."

"What do you remember about that morning?"

"Not much. I remember getting up to make coffee. It was extremely early, so I was trying not to wake Edie up and went to the kitchen. I had a nightmare and knew there wasn't a prayer for my going back to sleep. I thought I let Beacon out, but I have a vague memory of him barking. He rarely barks and the next thing I knew I was in the hospital. That's about it."

"Alright, let's take it from there. I've been in touch with Dr. Trent and was able to gather some history from your stay at Averton Psychiatric Hospital. Have you had any return of the "hysterical blindness" or any problems, concerning it?"

"No, the blindness hasn't returned but the flashbacks have."

"Do you remember exactly when you regained your sight?"

"Of course, I do," Aaron said. "I haven't completely lost my memory. I was still at Averton. I'd spent a particularly rough night; one nightmare after another. It was as if someone opened the floodgates and there was no turning back. It was strange, I woke up the next morning and it was like it never happened. My blindness was completely gone. I think Dr. Trent was as surprised as I was. He's convinced my blindness was what my mind devised to give me the isolation it needed temporarily to facilitate healing from my survival guilt. It's strange, but I've finally quit worrying about it returning. It happened one day when I was in the field. I left to go relieve myself in the woods and I realized I'd forgotten my KA-BAR. I went back to get it. I couldn't have been gone but a few minutes when I saw Hank, my best friend go down just as I walked out. He tripped over a tree root and fell face down on a land mine. It exploded and

71

he died immediately. It's a good thing he didn't survive because his mother wouldn't have been able to recognize him. I sustained some minor burns to my face and was knocked out temporarily. I don't remember being put in a Medivac or anything else until I woke up in the hospital."

"What is a KA-BAR?"

"A KA-BAR is a knife with a seven-inch blade and wrapped leather handle; it can be used for everything from cutting down brush to cleaning your fingernails, opening rations, or defending yourself. It made its first appearance with the Marines in World War II in 1943. When the Vietnam War broke out, the military made the KA-BAR a standard issue item. The USMC and USN removed their stamp and replaced it with the US stamp. It's invaluable to a soldier and he makes sure he never lets it out of his sight."

"It was shortly after I regained my sight, that I ran into Edie, who is now my wife at Averton Hospital. She was there to pick up her sister, and how do you explain meeting your soulmate and deciding you want to live again? I met her when I was still blind. I think I fell in love with her voice but didn't know it then. I was really in a bad place. I found out she was a famous singer and bought a bunch of her albums. Maybe it was a pipe dream, but I knew somehow, we would be together one day. I listened to her every day and went to sleep every night listening to her music. I thought when Edie and I got married everything would be okay and the nightmares would be behind me forever. My vision was back and for a while, it was one long honeymoon. But then the damn demons came back. I'm afraid to go to sleep because of the horrible nightmares. It's like being in 'Nam all over again. As if that's not bad enough, hardly a day goes by that something doesn't freak me out and I'm back in that hellhole again. If I hear a car backfire, it's all I can do not to hit the floor. The other night, Edie was popping popcorn on the stove, and I had to leave the room. We went to a nursing home last month to see her grandmother and the underlying smell of urine and disinfectant made my knees go weak."

"What do you think made you have such a strong reaction to the smell of urine?"

"Death, it's something we smelled every day. You know, when the body dies, the bladder and bowels immediately let go. The Grim Reaper has no mercy on you or regard for your dignity. You never forget that smell."

"You seem angry. Beacon seems in tune with your emotions as well. Did you bring him back from Vietnam with you?"

"I did, but no thanks to Uncle Sam. Beacon was a gift from my dad. Uncle Sam could care less about our working dogs in 'Nam."

"Why in the world would you say such a thing? That doesn't sound right. I have read great things about our military war dogs. They are extremely loyal to their handlers and have even sacrificed their lives for them."

"That is true, but when their handlers get killed or their tour is up, they immediately are passed off to another handler. If their injuries or age prevents them from working anymore, our government views them as government issue and they are either euthanized or left behind to fend for themselves. John Q public has no idea what a horrible end might come to them. Unfortunately, the Vietnamese view dogs as food. If they happen to catch them, sometimes they are killed and eaten."

"Why can't their handlers take them home with them?"

"It has never been allowed. I had a friend whose tour ended ahead of mine. He said he tried everything he could to take his dog home with him, but was told emphatically no. He finally gave up but was devastated. After 1969, the president passed a bill that service dogs would be treated as veterans, but my buddy was never able to locate his dog. Beacon was a gift from my dad from Spirit Angels, a canine service farm near the hospital I stayed in before I came home. Service dogs were raised there and trained specifically for our military who had special needs from their injuries. He was brought to me in the hospital, and we did my therapy together. We also did service training together; we bonded right away so Beacon was a snap to learn from. You're right about his being in tune with my emotions. He is more than a service dog and sleeps on the floor by our bed. He is very devoted. In the past he woke me up whenever I had a nightmare; still does but I thought the nightmares were over. I am angry most of the time. I was raised in a Christian-based home where God was ever present, and I still struggle to justify all the killing because of it."

"Of course, but don't the scriptures also speak of wars and rumors of wars? Isn't killing, in wartime different?"

"But do the scriptures mention enjoying it? I am a third-generation soldier to fight for my country. During training, we are programmed to become "killing machines." When you sit beside a comrade at breakfast and thirty minutes later see his head blown off, the "killing machine" takes over." All you can think of is revenge. I don't remember feeling remorse at those times, just euphoria for making the enemy pay. When I got the chance, I went to see our company chaplain and his suggestion was, "Hell, let's just go out and get drunk, *it doesn't matter."*

"Aaron, I'm so sorry. You mentioned you had a nightmare the morning Edie called an ambulance. Are you able to remember anything at all about the nightmare?"

"Vaguely, but it didn't make any sense. I was reliving a horrible day. My team and I walked into one of the VC's flimsy buildings if you could call it that. The front was in shambles, barely a shell of itself. I was canvasing the inside perimeter for Charlie. I had just removed my helmet to wipe away the sweat and dirt from my face, when I was able to give my men the "all clear," and realized something

74

was dripping on my head. It was blood and it was coming from a hole in the ceiling. When I went outside to check it out, it was one of my men lying on his back on the bullet-ridden roof; his body was still warm. His body looked like a human dart board from Charlie's bayonet and all the bullets."

"Now we're getting somewhere. Aaron, do you realize hearing the dripping coffee might have thrown you into a flashback of the dripping blood falling on you, and the man you lost from your team? I heard you were on your hands and knees that morning repeatedly banging your head on the cabinets in a trance of sorts. No wonder your recall is vague."

Aaron looked horrified. "You could be right, but how do I control these flashbacks? I flip out. I don't remember doing that. What does my banging my head on the cabinets have to do with my memory of that day in 'Nam? If I can't remember, what else have I done that I don't remember? I'm terrified my flashbacks will affect my job. My marriage could come apart at the seams. I'm married to the sweetest and most beautiful woman only dreams are made of, and most of the time I feel so numb I don't feel like I'm even alive. I know Edie loves me but how long will she be able to? I love her more than life itself but sometimes I just want to isolate myself from everyone, even Edie. It makes no sense to me. Am I deliberately or subconsciously sabotaging my marriage?"

"In my professional opinion, I don't think you are Aaron. When your mind flashes back to the horrific things you've experienced, it is so painful, that you automatically go into a trance or a self-destructive behavior mode; anything to escape the pain. As horrible as your memories are you did escape on some level by shutting down through your temporary blindness for a brief time. Oftentimes, when the memory of something is so horrific, we develop self-destructive behaviors because we have so much survival

75

guilt and an overpowering need to punish ourselves. Your feeling numb happens a lot to our veterans. It is a form of protection the brain devises. It's definitely not healthy but subconsciously you think if you can't feel, then if someone dies or leaves you it won't hurt as much. As frightening as it sounds, I think everything you have told me so far is what we call PTSD (Post Traumatic Stress Disorder). Once the floodgates opened as you said, you didn't need the blindness anymore. As painful as it sounds, you are finding your way back."

"Think about it. The narrative was "Don't feel, just kill." Before you even stepped on the battlefield you were taught to dehumanize the enemy by calling them, gooks, zipper heads, slant eyes, and any other terrible name that would make it easier to kill them. When World War I and World War II vets came home they were with their units and had two weeks on average with their spouses or families, courtesy of the government before they were dumped back into society."

"Not us, I don't have a clue what ever happened to my C.O. or my buddies. It haunts me."

"With all the political unrest about Vietnam, you must have felt like an outcast when you got home; by yourself I presume."

"Yes, one morning I was eating breakfast with the guys and the next day as soon as I was released from the hospital, my butt was immediately put on a plane. They put Beacon in the luggage carrier below. I only had my cane. I can only imagine what that was like for him. We'd never been separated since he was sent to me. I tried to take my seat and the woman next to me called me a "baby killer" and got up and moved. I didn't need to see her face to feel the hatred. It was almost tangible. You would have thought I was Lt. Calley, Jr."

"Ah, yes, I remember him well; Lt. Calley Jr., from the Mai Lai massacre. They made him a scapegoat, I'm afraid."

"Of course, they did. It didn't work. President Richard Nixon did what he could. The people back home didn't have a clue what was going on. How do you think that made me feel? Twelve months of fighting my ass off for my country and I find out no one cared; thought we were all a bunch of animals. Hell, even President Johnson used to say he wanted America to forget Vietnam and move on. So, tell me how do I do that? To whom do I talk? No one understands. Even Edie tries but I can't talk about it most of the time. I just want to forget."

"That's what we're going to work on. Sadly, we are ill-equipped to handle our boys coming home from a horrible war like Vietnam. It is a new frontier we are embarking on, and you and I will learn together. Our session is over for today, but I want you to do an exercise for me. I want you to start a journal. I don't want you to feel pressured to write every day. Think of it as a friend you would talk to like you are to me and write down how you are feeling. You might be surprised at what shows up. Bring your journal with you to your next session. It took a lot of courage for you to come here today; you have started on a journey, and you should be extremely proud of yourself."

"Like I have a choice," Aaron said glibly. "I'll see you next week." Beacon, still on sentry duty, got up and followed Aaron to the door, with his magnificent head down feeling his precious Aaron's sadness.

Chapter Twelve

"Amy, you look gorgeous. How are you? Where is Amanda? I was looking forward to seeing my niece." The girls decided they were overdue to meet for lunch and decided to catch up at Bentley's, their favorite restaurant.

"I'm sorry, I left her with the sitter. I have some errands to run after this. I'll bring her to see you soon, I promise. I'm doing well, believe it or not. I love my students. I'm enjoying the challenge of making history as exciting as I can and enticing my students to grasp it at the same time," Amy said. "Need I even ask about you? You look positively radiant. Married life agrees with you. How was the honeymoon?"

"It was like a dream. Paris is such a romantic city. All the books and stories we read as kids can't begin to do it justice. Can you imagine what Mother would say if she knew we went there for our honeymoon?"

"That's easy. She'd say something derogatory hoping to get a reaction out of you or at the very least ruin it. You know that. You've always needed her approval somehow. You must know by now that is impossible. You know how toxic she is. Look at you, Sis, you are a famous singer. You don't need her approval or anyone else's for that matter to validate who you are. You got where you are today all by yourself."

"Thank you, Amy. You can't know how much that means to me. I appreciate it. Actually, with God's help, I did have some lucky breaks and some wonderful people who were there early on and responsible for launching my career. Travis Perrin, my manager discovered me, thanks to Keith Sheffield, my boss, at his restaurant. I was singing at a few venues when I got the chance, but he knew Travis and invited him to hear me sing one night. The rest is history. Just think, if Aunt Susan hadn't paid for me to have voice lessons, none of it would have been possible.

You were right about visiting Mother. I was in tears when I left. Nothing ever changes. I'll always be a complete failure in her eyes. She hurt my feelings when I tried to give her a copy of my new album. She wouldn't even take it from me when I tried to hand it to her. I left it on that hideous chair she never lets anyone sit on."

Amy laughed. "You're right, nothing ever changes. You know that was deliberate but for all you know she might have played it as soon as you left. You forget that is how she elevates her sad ego by hurting others. Have you started therapy yet? I know how you always swore that wasn't your cup of tea, but it has saved my life."

"You'll be pleased to know I have made an appointment. Aaron has a new therapist and I think he's making progress."

"I can't imagine. Aaron is such a special person. It's unbelievable what those guys went through. How do you cope with the emotional pain he carries from Vietnam?"

"It breaks my heart, but I love him and pray all the time he'll be able to have peace one day. What about you? Are you still seeing Dr. Trent?"

"No, I don't need to be on my meds anymore if you can believe it. I do go to a therapist about once a month and I suppose at some point I could drop my therapy, but it makes me feel grounded somehow."

"That makes perfect sense to me. We never knew from one minute to the next what was going to happen when we were kids. I know I never felt safe. Amy, I hope someday you'll be able to talk about it. Where did you go for all those years? I even hired a private detective to find you. I thought you were dead."

"I'm so sorry sis, but I just can't talk about it yet. I can say I was so lost; it was like being dead. I'm so glad you found Aaron. Someday, I'll find someone like that."

"I don't want you to feel pressured. I can wait until you're ready. Meeting Aaron changed my life. We're even talking about having a family." The waiter brought them their Caesar salads and they waited politely for him to finish serving.

"Oh, that's so exciting. I could be an aunt and Amanda could have a cousin to play with. What about your singing? It might be a challenge juggling a career, a husband, and a baby. Knowing you, you will figure it out. I forgot to tell you, I've met someone and I'm authoring a book."

"You've met someone, and you're authoring a book? That is amazing and you're just now telling me? You are glowing. What wonderful news. How did you meet him? I want to hear everything."

"He teaches art at the same school I teach. He's been divorced for three years, has no children, and is nice. We just started dating. He loves the theatre too. He is gorgeous, tall, and such a good listener. He's great with Amanda and she adores him. He knows my whole story about the rape and my stay at Averton. He is such a good man."

"I'm so happy for you Amy. Tell me about this book. I know when we were kids, you were always writing poetry. Is it a memoir? I always said if we ever wrote a book about our lives, it would be a best seller."

"Absolutely not; I have no desire to relive that pain. I've worked too hard to put that behind me. It's a romance mystery that takes place in the nineteenth century."

"What's the title? What's it about?"

"*The Sword Cuts Both Ways* and it takes place during the Civil War. It begins with a young couple who buy an older house and remodel it, and they find the diary of the original owner of the house. It is a complete accounting of the secret romance of a southern girl with a Yankee soldier in Baton Rouge, LA. right in the middle of the Civil War." Julia Ann Meriweather is caught up in the romance of it and sets out to learn everything she can about the original owner and the history of the house she has just bought.

"Amy, I'm so proud of you. I'm speechless; you've accomplished so much in such a short time. You've finished school, gotten your degree, are raising a beautiful child on your own, landed a dream teaching job and now you're writing a book."

"Thank you, Sis. I appreciate that. I'm only about halfway through it but it's always been a dream of mine. I do feel as if my life is full now and it's a good feeling. Tell me, are you still planning on seeing Mother again and chasing that relationship?"

"I don't think so. I think you're right about Mother. She's gotten even more malicious since Edwin has died but I still wish she cared how well my career has taken off. I told you how it was when I went to her house. I still can't believe she didn't even care enough to come to our wedding. I'm the one who is different and wants more now. Amy, do you remember when we were kids and I got lost in that horrible blizzard?"

"Of course, I do, you were terrified. I felt so bad for you. I was so mad at Ms. Mendelson. She held me up talking about her silly cat and I was late getting outside to meet you and walk you home. They called Dad but they didn't tell me. It was horrible, but at least we could have been together until Dad found us."

"But I don't understand. I remember every horrible detail, even being unable to see my hands in front of my face, at some point but I don't remember how I got out or home. That frightens me."

"That's because you were so traumatized you just zoned out, I guess. You were only six. When I found you, you were standing in one spot with your arms out covered with snow. There was so much snow on that awful coat Caroline bought you, that you couldn't tell what color it was. You looked like a snowman. Your glasses were covered with snow. Dad finally picked us up and you didn't say a word for hours. Mother found out about it and wanted to take you to a psychiatrist. She was convinced you were in trauma, and it was all Dad's fault for not picking us up early before the blizzard. Dad squelched that right away and it was out of her hands. Maybe you should have seen someone. By evening you came around, but you never brought it up. Does it bother you? You should bring it up with your counselor. If you are still carrying that memory around, then it's important and a counselor will help you work through it.

"It bothers me that after I got lost everything after that until the next day is a complete blank Maybe you're right, it might be something I should share with my counselor. I do have a problem if I get lost. It's like a panic attack of the worst kind. I need to go Sis, but this has been so much fun. We need to do it more often. We can double date now that you have a boyfriend. I love you." She grabbed Amy and gave her a big hug. Amy returned the embrace. It was like they were kids again and the years they were apart had magically fallen away.

"So, Aaron, how have you been since our last visit? Have you started a journal yet?"

"Yes, but I don't write in it every day. Some days I'm just too raw. It's hard to say where I'm at right now. I'm enjoying my job as a flight instructor but still having nightmares. Edie said she woke up the other night to me straddling her, shaking her by her shoulders, and hollering we had to get out. I don't remember a thing about it. She said I lay back down when she told me to and never woke up. I think that's why I'm so exhausted all the time. Edie's always trying to get me to commit to a checkup."

"I don't see anything wrong with that. Your physical health is extremely important and has a direct impact on your mental health. What was her demeanor when she told you about your nightmare?"

"Edie is a trooper and of course, she is always empathetic, but how long is she going to put up with my crap? What if I hurt her when I'm in one of my crazy modes?"

"I can prescribe something for your anxiety if you like. Keep in mind you are in a healing mode right now. It could take years." You will never forget what you've been through. You will find a way to head off the nightmares eventually through therapy. In the meantime, it's important you get plenty of rest and you will develop your own particular way of coping when they do come. Are you sure you don't want me to write you a prescription?"

"No, I'm not ready for that yet. I saw too many *druggies* in 'Nam. Besides, aren't there side effects?"

"Yes, you're right. The side effects can be daunting. We'll wait awhile but I want you to keep me posted on what's going on, okay? Do you have any questions?"

"Just one, how can I be madly in love with my wife and still wish I were still in Vietnam killing the enemy? Sometimes after everyone has gone home, I sit in the parking lot at the airfield reminiscing about flying again, watching the planes take off, and simulators don't cut it for me. So, what is wrong with me?"

"Vietnam may have been a different life than you were used to here at home, but it became your life, just the same, however surreal, and violent it was. You are trying to live in this world now and learn how to juggle memories from your former life. Your memories will never leave you, I'm afraid as I said. You will learn to live with them eventually. One day you'll be able to fly again, focus on that. As I've said before, we will learn together as those of us in the medical field have only begun to study PTSD and what it has done to our boys coming home from the Middle East. In wars gone by, we called it "shell shock" and knew even less about it then. Sadly, our objective at that time was to let our boys rest a little, patch them up, and put them right back on the battlefield."

"That all sounds interesting, but the reality is I have to deal with my life now and give Edie the life she deserves. I see it's time for me to go. Come on, Beacon, let's go."

***

Chapter Thirteen

"Mrs. Carrington, Dr. Kensing will see you now."

"Please have a seat, Mrs. Carrington. I'm Dr. Kensing. Is it Weissman or Carrington?"

"I've kept my professional name Carrington, but I use both."

"What has brought you here to see me today?"

"I think I'm finally here for myself. I've spent most of my adult life worrying about my sister Amy when she was missing, and then when I did find her again, worrying about her mental health. She was missing for twelve years. She's doing well now; has finished school, has a great teaching job, is raising a child on her own, and Aaron, my husband is in therapy himself, so it's about time for me."

"Sounds like you have been so busy caring for others, you haven't taken time for yourself."

"You're probably right but I'm doing it now."

"And that is a step in the right direction for you. Tell me about your mother."

"My mother? That is so cliché. What does my mother have to do with anything? I'm here for myself. I know I have some work to do. Somedays I feel so out of it, it is exhausting to pull myself up emotionally. My career is everything to me and I don't want to do anything that will jeopardize it, so here I am."

"Edie, we are a combination of our experiences. Our parents and childhood serve as a foundation for the rest of our lives. They can be positive and nurturing or negative and fragmented. Through therapy, it is possible to reveal what effect they have on our lives and learn from it. If necessary, we can discover a great deal from the negative fallout and how to turn it around in our favor. Therapy can be one of the healthiest things you can do for yourself."

"What if the truth doesn't set me free, but instead binds me to my past? *'The past is never dead. It's not even past.'*

"I see you are a fan of William Faulkner. Let's hope we've learned a little more since then. Edie, we are not defined by our past any more than we are by our experiences. While they affect how we perceive the world, we still can choose the path we want to take. We are all so much more than that. Look at what you've accomplished with your career. Therapy only visits our past to help us untangle the knots and show us how far we've come. You are the one who does all the work. Think of me as your cheerleader."

"I hope you're right. I have no idea or know where to start."

"Let's start with your mom."

"Mother is how we addressed her. I don't ever remember addressing her as mommy or her telling us she loved us. I suppose she may have thought she did. She kept us clean and well-dressed. I'm sure my dresses were starched and ironed. She and my father divorced when I was four and Amy was ten or so. My dad remarried my stepmother, Caroline. She never wanted us. I think I knew that immediately."

"You sound fairly sure."

"My dad had custody of us, but she was always angry, and I heard them whispering a lot. I cried a lot for my mother, and I think Oovia resented that. On my first day of school, the teacher said, "Don't cry honey, your mother will come back and pick you up in a little while." When I said, 'She's not my mother,' I'm sure it must have hurt Caroline''s feelings and embarrassed her. It wasn't too long after that she gave my dad a choice, either her or us. He chose her. He took us to the same foster family we stayed with when he first filed for divorce, and we were made wards of the court. The Crain's were nice enough people, but we were devastated. Amy liked Caroline and Caroline wanted Amy. They had some sort of connection. I think I looked too much like my mother for Caroline to handle. My dad wouldn't hear of splitting us up, thank God, so off we went. Amy was more like a mother to me than a sister.

"How was Caroline otherwise?"

"She wasn't mentally ill like Mother was, but her anger was almost tangible. She didn't beat us or anything like that, but she seemed to find more fault with me than Amy for some reason. I missed my mother a lot. Maybe that enraged her. I stayed with an upset stomach and sometimes I couldn't eat. She had that "old school" mentality you had to eat everything on your plate no matter what. I remember one time in particular, it was a bowl of oatmeal. It had gotten cold, and she swore I was going to finish it no matter how long it took. My dad came home one day early for some reason. She put it in the refrigerator when he drove up and the next day, she made me eat it straight out of the refrigerator. I gagged a couple of times, but I got it down. I made it to the bathroom and threw it up."

"Did you tell your father?"

"Never, I was terrified of her. If I crossed her as she saw it, she knew how to punish me. I had a doll that was everything to me. I slept with it and dragged it everywhere. Once she took it away from me for a week. I was a basket case. I was five. Amy made me a cloth doll or bunny, not sure. It had floppy ears that couldn't stand up. She sewed it by hand, and I loved it. It was a funny-looking little thing, but I thought it was beautiful. I still have it. It saved the day. I slept with it every night and Bubbles when I got her back. I hid the doll Amy made under the mattress during the day. She didn't have a clue."

Eventually, we were returned to our mother and Edwin, her new husband. I think my father had a lot of guilt for putting us in a foster home. He said it would only be for a short time. It turned out to be almost three years. He didn't have the backbone to stand up to Caroline. He chose her over his children. For the life of me, I don't know how he got away with putting us in a foster home as the courts had already granted him legal custody of us. No one ever said anything, I guess. Things were certainly different then."

"How did you feel about your father putting you and your sister back in foster care?"

"I was shattered of course. I couldn't understand how he could abandon us like that."

"You seem angrier with your mother than your father. Do you know why that might be?"

"I'm not sure. Maybe I projected all the blame on Caroline so I wouldn't have to think about it. I always knew my father loved me and I never knew if my mother did. She played with our feelings like we were puppets on a string. As an adult, I knew my father was weak. I guess it was easier to forgive him than my mother and all she did to us."

"Do you know why your dad filed for divorce?"

"It was always the elephant in the room that was never discussed. I always had questions, but never got a definitive answer from my mother. Caroline, my stepmother, said my mother left us home alone while she went dancing and my father came home late one night, and we were by ourselves. I remember hearing loud voices at night. It wasn't hard to figure out they were fighting. It upset me but I didn't understand what was going on until it became obvious and then I was traumatized to be away from my mother. I struggled. I think I spent most of the first part of my childhood with an upset stomach. I was neurotic or at least I sure heard that I was often enough. Mother always threatened to take me to a psychiatrist. I was terrified. I think Amy compartmentalized it in her own way. I doubt if it was healthy, but we never talked about it as kids even to each other. I don't think I was aware things weren't right until we were taken away from Mother. I was so young. Amy had a better idea of what was going on since she was older. It seemed I was always alone. Amy was older enough that she was off playing with her friends. I always had my head buried in a book for as long as I can remember. Books were my friends and were always with me. I remember reading *Marjorie Morningstar* by Herman Wouk in junior high. It was quite an accomplishment as it was thick enough to use for a doorstop. As a result, I mispronounced words sometimes because if I didn't know the definition, I would look it up but never actually heard how it was pronounced and did the best I could. I was pretty shy, and it never occurred to me to ask for help. To this day I have worked hard to overcome what Amy and I missed by making it a practice to constantly stretch and grab extra continuing education hours any time the opportunity presented itself. College never seemed enough to me. Later, of course, when I started my singing career, it seemed I was always learning everything I could, piano lessons, voice lessons; whatever my aunt could afford until

I met Travis Perrin, my agent. My Aunt Susan was there for me emotionally and financially. I owe her everything."

I don't think Amy ever got over her anger with our mother. It wasn't until years later that I realized Amy had problems. She was only a junior in high school when she ran away, and no one knew where she was for a while. When she did come home, she and Mother barely spoke. A short time later she ran away again and married someone she hardly knew. When she left, I felt lost. "I've only learned recently most of what took place, from Amy since we've reconnected; her memories are so much clearer than mine."

"Were you raised by your mother and stepfather?"

"No, shortly after we returned to the States, my dad and Caroline were killed in a car accident. When Amy ran off and got married, we were still overseas. After we got back to the States I never went back with my mother after the funeral and lived with my aunt for a while until I started making enough money to strike out on my own. My Aunt Susan was so supportive of everything I did. She was the parent my mother could never be. Amy was still in Germany with her husband as his tour wasn't up yet when Dad and Caroline had their accident. It was only a few weeks after the funeral that Amy just disappeared. Her husband, Scott thought she was with us for the funeral. We thought she was back in Germany with her husband; Scott had no idea where she went." Edie painfully described the horrible day of the accident.

***

"I was just getting home from school, throwing my books on the bed in my room, and about to change my clothes when I heard the doorbell ring."

"Aunt Susan, what a nice surprise; what are you doing here?" Edie asked. "I need to call Mother and let her know you're here."

"There's something I need to tell you honey first. Sit down with me, okay?" Edie did not like her aunt's energy. She knew right away that Aunt Susan was upset about something and was at a loss how to tell her.

"Edie, I'm so sorry to tell you this but your father and Caroline have both been in a terrible car accident."

"Dear God, are they okay?" Edie jumped up and headed for the hall closet to grab a jacket.

Susan immediately jumped up and caught Edie pulling her into her arms, looked into her face, and said. "Edie, honey they're both gone. I'm so sorry. I've already notified Amy. Scott has put her on a plane. You are going to spend the night with me. You are welcome to stay with me as long as you like. Your mom has agreed it might be a good idea for a little while."

Edie was devastated; she was in shock. She loved their Aunt Susan, but her dad was her rock. If it weren't for Caroline, she would be living with her dad and not the pervert that her mother was married to. She knew she couldn't live with Amy and Scott because she recently learned they were having problems already. What was she going to do?

Edie struggled with the loss of her father every day. Even though Caroline made sure that the girls didn't live with them early on, she and her dad had managed to get together quite a bit and they were close. He wanted to hear about everything she was doing and told her many times she had the voice of an angel and to sing every chance she got. Despite her mother constantly berating her, that's exactly what she did. As young as she was, she realized her mother's hatred for her father was why she was always catching hell. Even though she knew, it still kept her in emotional turmoil.

At first, when she was small, she entered a lot of talent shows. When she went to Germany with her mother and stepfather, she had an opportunity to sing in a play on board the ship they were on. She sang Judy Garland's, *Somewhere Over the Rainbow*. The moment she walked on that stage and started singing she was hooked. When she looked out at the audience, she felt energized. When she finished, they clapped; it was exhilarating. She was ten years old.

"Mother, when we get back to the States, I want to take voice lessons."

"No, I see your dad has been filling your head with all kinds of pipe dreams again. You need to find other interests. There are far more lucrative paths you could choose to go down than singing and they all require taking your studies more seriously."

"Mother, I do take school seriously. I'm on the honor roll. I'm twelve now and will be in high school soon. I want to major in music when I go to college."

"How many times do I have to tell you, you're not "college material." Why would you even put yourself through something like that? You need to find someone who can support you and get married. This subject is no longer open for discussion. Now change your clothes and meet us upstairs in the dining room for dinner."

That's fine, she thought, she would get her dad to pay for her to take voice lessons. She was thirteen when her stepfather's tour of duty was finished, and they returned to the States. But of course, that never happened because when they got back to the States, her dad and Caroline were killed in an automobile accident, and she grabbed the opportunity to move in with her aunt. Edwin, her stepfather was getting more aggressive in his behavior towards her, and she knew after what happened to Amy, it would do no good to tell her mother. and was grateful she could move in with her Aunt Susan and her husband. Her mother didn't seem that concerned about it. She was probably relieved to get rid of her. She never told her aunt about Edwin because she wasn't sure what would happen. As much as she loved her aunt, she was beginning to develop some trust issues. Aunt Susan's husband never bothered her and seemed to be a nice person, but she steered clear of him and made sure if she was in the room with him, it was only when someone else was in the room with them.

Chapter Fourteen

Olivia, what is your problem? What have you got against Edie taking voice lessons? I'll pay for everything. You know how talented she is. After all those girls have been through and now losing their father. Voice lessons are the best thing that we could do for her now. It will get her mind off of things."

"You're just trying to undermine my authority like you always do. Everyone knows she is your favorite. It's not my fault you never had any kids of your own."

"Why would you even say such a thing? That's even low, for you. Honestly, Olivia, you can be so cruel."

"So do it then. I couldn't care less. I think you're wasting your money. Edie is too much like her father; she hasn't the backbone to follow through with anything. I'll give her a month."

Susan was seething from Olivia's cruelty but knew if she let her sister think for a minute she had the upper hand, she would change her mind just out of spite. She could only imagine how those girls had survived in that house as long as they had. It was a tossup who was more toxic, her sister or that fool she was married to. There was something about Edwin that made her skin crawl.

"Aunt Susan, I can't believe you did this. Does mother know?"

"You let me take care of my sister. God has given you a gift, and these voice lessons will hone your skills and open many doors for you. I believe in you and someday your mother will come around. If she doesn't, you still have a gift and need to follow your dream and I will support you 100 percent."

Thanks to her Aunt Susan, Edie began to follow her dream. Teresa Sheridan, her music teacher was a petite older lady and Edie fell in love with her immediately. She was thrilled Aunt Susan was able to find her and for the opportunity to pursue her dream. Ms. Sheridan was dedicated and all business but somehow felt comfortable with letting her students know she cared about them. Edie was ready to learn anything Ms. Sheridan could teach her. They were a perfect match. Three days a week Aunt Susan dropped her off at Ms. Sheridan's house and it was the highlight of her day She could hardly wait to get out of school and to practice.

"Okay Edie, let's get you on the piano for a while."

Edie was intimidated by the piano at first since she found it difficult to learn how to read music, but Ms. Sheridan was patient and supportive.

"Edie, are you taking my advice and observing good vocal hygiene? If you're as serious as I think you are, you'll want to make it a habit you stick to from now on. You have a precious gift my dear and you must protect that voice at all costs."

"Yes ma'am, I drink lots of water and stay away from dairy products and spicy food as much as I can. I've also been working on a song I'm writing."

"Wonderful! I would love to see it as soon as you finish it. I can help you with the notes if you like. Now, first things first. Let's hear what you've been practicing."

***

Discovered

The years rolled by; Edie was nineteen and still taking voice lessons and piano from Ms. Sheridan. She'd moved out of her Aunt Susan's house and got an apartment of her own, worked at a local upscale restaurant, and sang at different venues whenever she got the chance. She still had most of the inheritance her dad left her, so she was doing all right. One night, Sheffield's, the restaurant where she worked held a catered event for a small group of Mr. Sheffield's friends and he asked her to sing some numbers for the evening. Mr. Sheffield was very fond of Edie and had heard her sing before, knew she had a gift, and jumped at the chance to show her off. What Edie didn't know was that Keith Sheffield had a good friend in the music business and decided to give him a call. If he had to guess, he thought his friend would be impressed by her voice and stage presence. Edie loved the ambiance at the event and was thrilled that Mr. Sheffield thought of her and allowed her to perform in front of his friends.

"Edie, you look lovely as usual. I know you're going to dazzle us tonight with that voice."

"Thank you, Mr. Sheffield, I appreciate you giving me the opportunity." Edie decided on a lovely emerald, green sleeveless sheath of a shimmery material with a modest sweetheart neckline for the event. It made her green eyes pop. She chose to pull some of her dark hair up and the effect was stunning. People were dressed to the nines, and everyone seemed to be having a good time. Mr. Sheffield treated her more like a daughter and she thought a lot of him and hoped he and his guests would enjoy her music.

Edie sang *The Rose* and *Unchained Melody* to the small but receptive group and was pleasantly surprised by what an enthusiastic crowd they were. Afterward, she circulated a little, fixed herself a plate, and found an empty seat.

People were coming up to her and making requests for their favorite songs. She looked up and saw a tall, slender older gentleman with a tailored dark brown corduroy blazer and black jeans with a sharp crease coming towards her. He had a rugged, weathered look like he'd spent a lot of time in the sun, a full head of salt and pepper hair, and a big smile that explained the tiny wrinkles around his eyes. "Ms. Carrington, my name is Travis Perrin. Who in the world taught you to sing like that?" he asked extending his hand.

"It's been a lifelong dream of mine and I've been working at it since I was a little girl, singing every time I got the chance."

"Well young lady, it shows. You have an amazing voice as well as an excellent stage presence. That is something those of us in the music business are always looking for."

"Thank you, Mr. Perrin. I've been taking voice and piano lessons from Ms. Sheridan for a few years, and she has taught me a lot."

"Indeed! Please call me Travis. Keith and I go way back, and he tells me you work for him, and you are always ready to sing for any venue that might come up. I would like to propose a business deal to you. Is there somewhere we might talk with some privacy?

"Yes, maybe Mr. Sheffield will let us use his office."

"Of course, he will," he said. "Lead the way."

Edie was in shock. She felt as if she were in a dream and any minute she would wake up and it would just evaporate. They talked for hours. Mr. Perrin worked out some songs the following week so she could cut an album. He didn't tell her, but he was already formulating a contract in his head. He was getting old, and he wasn't going to let this one get away. You just didn't see raw talent like this every day. He had a knack for recognizing talent and she was on fire when she first walked on the stage, even before she opened her mouth to sing. She had a presence and had the audience in the palm of her hand the moment she opened

99

her mouth. It wasn't just because she was beautiful, it was a God-given gift; her beauty was an added bonus. When she sang, she didn't hold anything back and it was as if she conveyed that to her audience naturally. There was an instinctive unspoken exchange between them. Whatever she felt, they felt.

"Edie, your demo sounds great. I've sent it to some of my friends with radio stations of their own. You have quite a following already. My friends tell me their phones are ringing non-stop, wanting to know all about the girl with the sultry voice. How would you like to come to Memphis with me to my studio? I've been talking to my lawyers, and I would like to sign you up to work for me. You have a great deal to offer with that voice and natural stage presence. You have a raw talent as we say in the music business, and I think we would make a great team; you, me, and EMI. You have the potential to go as far as you want and I'm just the man who can make it happen. What do you say?"

Edie was more than overwhelmed. She couldn't believe what was happening; it felt surreal. "Mr. Perrin, I mean Travis, it's the chance of a lifetime but I still need to make plans. I can't just drop everything. I have responsibilities here. I would need to give Keith notice. Ms. Sheridan will not be happy about me interrupting my voice lessons. And to be perfectly honest, I'm not comfortable signing a contract without having someone with a legal background of some kind go over it with me."

"Edie, I completely understand. Don't give Keith another thought. I've already talked to him, and he is thrilled for you. If it will make you feel better, you can pick a lawyer of your choice to sit down with us to go over the contract with you. My guys are overnighting the contract to me. Whether you decide to sign with us or not, I will pay him for his time before we ever leave. As for Ms. Sheridan, I will pay for you to have your own voice coach. I appreciate your loyalty to her, but there is a whole new life waiting for you out there. A voice coach is an important part of the team. You will learn a different way to sing and how to protect your voice. Once you start going on tours, it can be grueling and exhausting for your voice, so it is crucial to have a good voice coach. I'll be here for three more days so I hope you will be able to give me an answer by then. People don't get an opportunity like this every day and I'm grateful my friend Keith gave me a call. The rest is up to you."

Travis felt a slight twinge of guilt for giving Edie the rush, but it was for his business, and he knew in his bones she was going to be famous.

Things started happening fast after that. Edie's Aunt Susan and Ms. Sheridan were naturally skeptical of Travis Perrin. They both loved her and were protective of her, to say the least. She was only nineteen and what did any of them know about this man with his fancy tweed blazers and jeans with a crease? Edie's Aunt Susan finally agreed to put her on a plane to Memphis after reading Mr. Perrin the riot act and what she would do to him if any harm came to one hair on Edie's head. He promised Edie would call every night and keep her apprised of what was going on. In the meantime, Aunt Susan would contact the lawyer her family used, "thank you very much," and get all the particulars before Edie signed anything. As Travis mentioned, Mr. Sheffield was thrilled for her, had a permanent grin pasted on his face, and was proud as a peacock for the role he played in the whole thing.

Chapter Fifteen

Memphis

Edie fell in love with Memphis and all its venerable charm. It was an exciting city and growing exponentially. She was beyond impressed with Mr. Perrin's studio. It was massive and his staff were the epitome of professionalism. She had never sung anywhere before with the quality of equipment his studio offered, backing her up.

"Edie, I'm Art McBay, I'm so glad to meet you. I'll be your new voice coach. We're all looking forward to working with you. To her surprise, they were all kind and went out of their way to make her feel at home. Travis and I plan to take you to dinner tonight and go over what your week with us will be like. After we give you the nickel tour of our studio and send out for some lunch, we're going to give you the opportunity to check out your room at the hotel, get settled, and unwind a bit before tonight. How does that sound?"

"It sounds great to me," Edie said. "Thank you." She hoped she didn't sound as ecstatic as she felt. She felt like she was in the middle of a beautiful dream and any minute she would wake up and be back at Mr. Sheffield's wondering where her next gig was coming from.

She never dreamed Travis had registered her at the Peabody Memphis Hotel. The ambiance was breathtaking. She loved the elegance of the lobby and just missed seeing the legendary Peabody Ducks go through their routine. The hotel staff was the epitome of professionalism and treated her like royalty. Her room was elegant and spacious. After she called her Aunt Susan to let her know she'd arrived, Edie decided she would stretch out on the inviting king-size bed and close her eyes for a couple of minutes. The next thing she knew the clock on the wall showed she had been asleep for two hours. She couldn't believe it.

Dinner with Travis and Art, her new voice coach was an event in itself. It was obvious she was being given the red-carpet treatment but between the two of them, they ordered enough food for someone who hadn't eaten in two days. Everything was delicious but at the risk of hurting their feelings she raised both hands. "Guys, I surrender. I can't eat another bite. I have to watch my figure you know."

"We know; your svelte figure is another one of your assets, Edie. We wanted your first day in Memphis to be memorable. How was your stay in the Peabody?" Travis asked.

It was wonderful. The hotel is so elegant. I just missed seeing the legendary Peabody ducks.

"I was afraid of that. We'll work hard and try to send you back early one day this week so you can. It's something to see. You'll have to visit their rooftop as well. It's breathtaking! You can see the city's skyline and you've never seen a sunset like from the top of Peabody's rooftop.

"The Peabody Hotel was built in 1925. In 1940, Bellman Edward Pembroke, a former circus animal trainer offered to work with the ducks. He trained them in the legendary duck march to the fountain they do every day to this day. Sorry to ramble on but the Peabody is one of my favorite hotels."

"Okay Travis, she's mine now. Trust me, we will get to work first thing bright and early in the morning. We'll send a car for you at seven." Art said.

"Thank you, it has been like a dream but I'm ready to go to work."

Edie knew from Ms. Sheridan that one's voice was a precious commodity and how important rest, diet, etc. were but she was learning that there was a vast difference between a voice teacher and a voice coach.

"Okay Edie, I know you're anxious to show us what you've got. You can rest assured; you wouldn't even be here if Travis didn't believe in you. My job is to hone those skills you already have and give you some new ones so you can present the best possible version of yourself to your audience. When I'm through, chances are you'll discover a part of yourself you never knew," Art said. "You already have excellent posture in your favor," That's one thing she thought silently she could thank her mother for. It was drilled into both of their heads from childhood. "Posture is extremely important in the music business. Trust me, your voice will thank you. Today, I'm going to show you some voice exercises to warm up your vocal cords and folds. It is no different than how a runner prepares for his next race. It's something you should do every day to improve and strengthen them. Maybe Ms. Sheridan already did this with you, but I doubt if she comes close to being the task master I am. We are also going to learn about diction, sadly sometimes one of the most overlooked tools. If you have any limitations at all with your voice, your sentences won't be heard by your audience. Something as simple as not taking enough breaths before getting your words out will cause your sentences to trail off and your audience will not be able to hear you. I don't want to overwhelm you with anything else right now, but I think you will be pleasantly surprised by the improvement it will make in your singing. Now let's get to work.

Art McBay wasn't kidding when he referred to himself as a taskmaster. At first, Edie found him to be intimidating. While she understood the necessity for the voice exercises, they were grueling. When she finally did get the chance to sing, he would make her go over it, over and over until she got it right. "Repetition equals perfection, Edie. Nothing less is acceptable," was his mantra. She had to admit when he was finally satisfied, she was surprised at how well she sounded. She worked hard and she couldn't believe how fast time went by in the studio. Art pushed her but he knew what she was capable of and wouldn't settle for anything but her best and was impressed with her work ethic. She never complained and never asked to stop until he was ready. She worked hard and a week stretched to three and then she had been in Memphis for three months.

Finally, they had an album, *Edie Carrington, Sheer Magic*, and Travis was busy doing his magic. When it hit the charts and made number one, she was in shock.

"Edie, you made it girl." Art said, grabbing her, twirling her around, and passing her to Travis.

Edie, are you okay? You don't look so good. Congratulations on a job well done. I'm so proud of you. Take a few days off, go home for a visit, and then we'll get back to work. You're about to go on your first tour, young lady."

Edie was afraid any minute she would wake up and it would all be a beautiful dream. In the meantime, she was going to enjoy the ride and couldn't wait to see what was next.

"

Chapter Sixteen

Dr. Kensing

"So now we have an important piece of the puzzle; what an exciting way to have been discovered and launch your career. It's what dreams are made of."

"Edie, hear me out," Dr. Kensing said. "When you were separated from your mother at four, and your dad at seven you were in a crucial stage of your development. Three to four is one of the most crucial of a child's formative years and when a separation like that occurs at such a young age, a child loses those years forever, and it has a direct effect on their emotional development. The female brain doesn't reach full development until twenty-one. That should give you some idea of how important a healthy and safe environment is to a young child. Then your dad, the only stable influence in your life died in an accident years later. I have an idea you came here today searching for something specifically."

"I have no idea what that could be."

"Why do you think you're here?"

"I'm not sure. I know I have everything I ever wanted. I have a successful career, I am married to my soul mate, the most loving man I've ever met. We have even talked about having a family someday so what is wrong with me? I'm always waiting for something to ruin it; the proverbial axe to fall. I agonize regularly about something taking away my singing career or losing Aaron. Why can't I just be happy and let the past go?"

"First of all, you don't have to be here, but you chose to be. That sounds to me like you decided it was the right thing to do for yourself. Therapy is a good place to find the answers you're looking for. You mentioned your husband is in therapy?"

"Yes, Aaron is a veteran of the Vietnam War and suffers from PTSD. Therapy does seem to be helping him. Initially, he would never talk about anything he went through before but now I notice he brings up certain things on his own. While it is an honor and a responsibility to be trusted with that kind of confidence, I listen and pray he doesn't read the shock on my face. My beautiful, sweet Aaron; my heart aches for the horrible things he has gone through."

Let's get back to your mother. It sounds like your self-esteem was constantly under siege."

"It was. I was seven or eight when our dad sent us back to Mother and Edwin, my stepfather. Growing up and being told I was "slow" was like starting with a stacked deck. It didn't matter I had really good grades, I only absorbed the negative. When I was younger in school, a lot of times I knew the answer when the teacher would ask a question but was so insecure, I would never raise my hand. When I got older, of course it was I wasn't "college material" so I had better get married and have kids. When I mentioned it years later to my dad, he was livid and said it was a crock, that I developed at the same pace as any child, sometimes way ahead of the curve. By that time, I'm afraid the die had already been cast."

"That is unfortunate. Look at what you have managed to accomplish on your own. You are a famous singer and are on the front cover of every magazine. Young girls try and emulate your look, your essence. You are a beautiful and gifted woman, Edie."

"Thank you, Dr. Kensing."

"I see you aren't too comfortable receiving compliments. What goes through your mind when someone compliments you, Edie?"

"Initially, I enjoy it but then I start sabotaging it by substituting it with the garbage I've heard all my life. It seems to be automatic. I've learned to thank the person and hide how feel but sometimes I think it's harder when I do get compliments. What's so sad is we got mixed messages from our mother. I remember when I was in grade school, she surprised me once by making light-colored drapes and a matching valance for my room and then crocheting elaborate costumes for small dolls representing different countries and attaching them to the curtains by their massive skirts. It must have taken her hours just making outfits for all the dolls, let alone the drapes. I loved it. She is an excellent seamstress. Christmas was always an extravaganza with an obscene amount of presents. When we were little, she would take our older dolls, and give them new hair and new clothes. We never even knew they were missing. Of course, we loved it. She seemed obsessed with painting portraits of me but would paint my eyes blue instead of green. Everyone says I bear a strong resemblance to her. Maybe she was unconsciously painting herself in her youth. One Christmas I made her a lounging skirt/slacks. I thought they turned out pretty well. The very next time I went for a visit, she had taken them apart and made them into slacks."

"Why do you suppose she painted your eyes the wrong color?"

"Probably because she was jealous of the relationship I had with my dad, and she hated him for getting custody of us. Of course, his eyes were green and hers are blue."

"You do realize your mother was extremely ill, don't you? She controlled you and your sister by keeping you both on an emotional roller coaster."

"I do now, but I remember running to Amy for comfort when I got upset which was a lot."

"I think we've covered a tremendous amount of territory today, Edie. I'm impressed that you are willing to do the work right out of the gate. I'd like to see you again in a couple of weeks if you can manage it with your schedule."

Edie was deep in thought when she left Dr. Kensing's office. She felt he was sincere and wanted to help but was suddenly drained and couldn't wait to get home. When she pulled into the driveway, Aaron came out with Beacon trailing behind him to help if she had any packages.

"How was your session honey?"

"Exhausting. Honey, I'm so sorry, I completely forgot to stop at the store on the way home."

"Don't worry about it. I don't think we'll starve before tomorrow. If you make a list for me, I can pick up some things on my way home from work tomorrow. I may even be able to sneak off a little early, depending on how many students I have."

Edie threw her arms around Aaron's neck. "Thank you so much. You have no idea how much I appreciate it."

"Oh, but I do. Don't forget I'm in therapy too. This is a first for you. Trust me, it can be draining. I'm so proud of you. It takes a lot of courage to open that door. Just know, we can do it together. I'm here anytime you need a sounding board."

Walking into the house holding hands, Edie was totally surprised to see Aaron had fixed supper and what a spread he had set out. No wonder Beacon was so excited. The smells were all but making him drool. Edie was so touched by his gesture that she had to fight off the tears. Beacon sprinted to the dining room, following his nose, and somehow tripped over his own big feet and flipped end over appetite. They were hysterical laughing until Edie stopped when she noticed Aaron started choking and seemed to be struggling to catch his breath.

"Aaron, are you okay?" He sat down, and she didn't like his color. He neglected to mention the room was spinning for him and he felt weak but was trying to hide it from Edie.

"I'm fine honey. That silly dog is a laugh-a-minute, isn't he? Grab your plate and give me a second. Everything is in the kitchen. I'm right behind you. You must be starved." Aaron hoped Edie hadn't noticed he was hanging back to give himself time to regain his strength enough to stand on his weak legs. It was probably a sugar crash and he tried to remember if he had eaten that morning.

One night, as they were settling in, they were still basking in the afterglow from making passionate love. Edie was getting out of the shower and drying off when she heard a loud crash. Running into the bedroom, she saw Aaron in a heap on the floor by the bed with Beacon hovering over him like a helicopter unsure where to land or what to do.

"Beacon, come on, give me a break. I'm okay." He said, trying to get up. Poor Beacon was still nudging Aaron and licking his face until he realized Aaron was conscious.

"What happened? Are you okay?"

"I'm fine. You know what a klutz I am. I tripped over my own feet somehow. Kissing her, he said. "My turn, you just about killed me, woman," he said, heading for the shower.

Edie noticed Aaron weave to the right as if he were struggling for his balance. Something was wrong and she wasn't buying his sweeping it under the rug either.

"Aaron, you need to see a doctor, baby. Just getting up shouldn't cause you to be out of breath like this, let alone pass out."

"Come on, honey. I had terrible allergies as a kid. My electrolytes could be low or maybe it's asthma. You showed me no mercy tonight, you know."

"You've lost this argument. I'm making you an appointment for first thing Monday morning."

Aaron knew once Edie dug her feet in, there was no changing her mind.

"I guess I'm going to the doctor, Beacon. Momma's the boss."

The doctor wasn't a word in Beacon's vocabulary, but he cocked his head politely to the side anyway, trying to understand what his beloved Aaron was telling him.

***

"Amy, I'm so glad you called me, and we were able to get together. I've had you on my mind a lot lately," she said, giving her sister a huge hug."

"Is that your car in the driveway or Aaron's?"

"It's mine. Aaron is at the airfield, why?"

"I've never mastered getting behind the wheel. It's city buses or cabs for me. I guess I've been in awe ever since we've gotten back together that you have been able to circumvent your fear of driving."

"You too? You were already gone when I was in the middle of driving education, and one day I drove by the house with Mr. Jenkins, the Driver's Ed teacher. Mother and Edwin were in the front yard working on her flowerbeds, and I was so excited, I honked and waved. She looked right at us and then turned around showing me her back. The same day, when I got home, she made me drop driver's ed. Of course, I got an incomplete. She said it was too dangerous, and I didn't have the reflexes for it. I drive, despite it but sometimes the traffic freaks me out."

"The old "no reflexes" mantra; how well I remember. Edie, you know it was the ranting of a sick person. Don't forget she never drove herself and was terrified to get behind the wheel. Kudos to you that you didn't let it stop you."

"I don't know about all that. Fighting the fight all the time can be exhausting. It requires constantly tuning the tapes out. Please, sit down. Edie was thrilled they could get together. Aaron was at the airfield, and she had just gotten off tour for a week.

Amy jumped when she sat down and one of Beacon's squeaky babies went off under the sofa cushion. "What do we have here?" she said giggling. Beacon came out to join them with a silly look on his face, sat down, and tenderly took his baby when Amy handed it to him. "I didn't think you'd be here big boy. I thought you'd be with your daddy." Beacon's face lit up like a Christmas tree when she mentioned his hero.

"It is rare. They're inseparable but today he is going to be monitoring some of his students on their flying skills, and federal regulations don't allow canines to be in the cockpit. In the real world, Beacon is not recognized as his service dog anymore in some places. I don't think Aaron is comfortable talking about his PTSD when a question comes up but technically, he is still his service dog. It's ridiculous anyone would ever question that just because his disability isn't visible anymore."

"I agree. Aaron shouldn't ever have to deal with that. Beacon has a harness identifying him as a service dog anyway."

"You're right. Fortunately, it rarely comes up. Maybe Aaron's therapy will help him feel better about talking about it eventually. Aaron is flying again and there are going to be a lot more people milling around on the grounds today while he's in the air. Aaron is paranoid about putting Beacon in a situation where he could be stolen. He adores that dog and it's mutual. I shudder to think what would happen if anything happened to Beacon. They dote on each other."

"I don't blame him. They have a special bond. Edie, I've been thinking a lot about our conversation the last time we had lunch at Bentley's. I think I'm ready to tell you what happened to me while I was missing."

"Sis, I don't want you to feel pressured in any way. I respect your reticence. Whenever you're ready is fine with me. I'm just thrilled to have you in my life again."

"No, I'm ready. Not that it's an excuse, but I was so lost then. Remember when Edwin came into my room years ago? I was terrified. I really should have seen a therapist because it traumatized me for so many reasons. Edwin was after me for years, but I'd managed to steer clear of him somehow. I was studying in my room and had fallen asleep on the bed. I'm sure he knew Mother was out and I woke up with him pawing me. If it wouldn't have been for Skippy scratching on the door and whining it would have been all over. The coward took off. Of course, he threatened if I told anyone, he would send me away to a sanitarium and I'd never see you or Mother again. I did tell Mother and she didn't believe me or said she didn't. She accused me of having a crush on Edwin and inappropriately flirting with him. I was horrified. How could she even say something like that? When it was time to get back on the train, as soon as we got to Munich, Carrie and I skipped school and checked into a hotel. In two days, we were broke and Edwin came and got me. The ride home was horrible. Nothing was ever mentioned; like it never happened. Between Edwin and Mother, I felt like I was going crazy. I made a few surface cuts on my wrists and thought Mother would realize how upset I was and believe me. Instead, she signed me into a sanitarium. I think she wanted to remove me from her life. I only spent two nights there, but it did a number on my mind. You were so young; I don't know how much you remember."

"I remember it all. I didn't understand everything, but I was sick with worry about you, and I was lost when you ran off to get married. The pig never changed. He did the same thing to me. One night he and Mother were out dancing and hitting all the nightclubs, and I heard them when they came in. A few minutes later he came into my room and was crawling across the foot of the bed. I turned on the light. He was only in his underwear. I was terrified. I was only thirteen. I told him to get out of my room or I would tell Mother. It was awful. I could hear my voice shaking. He kept telling me to turn the light off, but I didn't. He was livid but he left. When I told Mother, she said he told her he had too much to drink, got confused on the way back from the bathroom, and thought he was in their room. He never came into my room again, but I was terrified he would until the day I moved to Aunt Susan's. I always put a chair against my door so I would hear him if it happened again. She stayed with him until he died, can you believe it? How does a mother do that?"

Oh, Sis, I'm so sorry. I wish I had been there for you. I only had a few dates with Scott when we ran off and got married. I thought he was sympathetic to what I'd been through. Turns out, he was a classic abuser. Why didn't I see that before we were married? It seemed everything out of his mouth started with, 'Don't you ever, I better not see you.' He would beat me for whatever trumped-up charge he could come up with. Sometimes, he would start if dinner wasn't ready when he got home. I know mother thought I was still mad at her, or you wondered why I didn't visit more often. Most of the time I was hiding out, trying to heal from a black eye or bruises; one time even a broken arm. Finally, I knew on some level if I didn't get out, he would kill me. When Aunt Susan called me about Dad and

Caroline, I came back home for the funeral as you know. Afterward, when you and Aunt Susan dropped me off at the airport, I knew I might never get an opportunity like that again. Scott wouldn't be looking for me for a day or so. I was sick about leaving you behind but didn't care if I ever saw Mother again and I was running for my life. I told myself when I got a job I would come and get you. It was rough. I got a job right away but quitting in my junior year didn't give me many options. Waiting tables didn't pay anything. Even with tips, it was rough. I met more duds but at least none of them beat me. It never helped with the loneliness. The years went by. I managed to finish high school and get my GED at night. I was a legal secretary for a prestigious law firm and babysat for my boss's kids a couple of times. He and his wife had some nice apartments and they let me rent one for a price I could afford. I even managed to enroll at the university to start working on my degree so I could teach one day. My boss gave me a generous raise but with tuition and my books, I was always living from payday to payday. Despite this, things were getting better for me. One night I was working late. I was walking home from the bus stop when someone jumped me, took my purse, and dragged me into an alley. He had a friend waiting in the alley. He threw my purse at him and pulled me further into the alley and raped me. They both did. The rest is a blur. I guess I left my body as a coping skill because I don't remember much else and hope I never do. Thank God, Mr. Canton, my neighbor saw me at the police station and recognized me. Even a lot of my stay at Averton is a blur. Dr. Trent believes our reunion was the catalyst that brought me back and I'm sure it was part of God's plan. The timing is so like God. However, nothing could have prepared me for finding out I was pregnant as you can imagine. Having Amanda has filled a void in my life I could have never dreamed. Most people wouldn't understand it, but God does and that's what's important. I worked extremely hard in therapy, and I think I've been able to forgive Mother or at least let go of the rage I carried for so long. Seeing her again is an entirely separate thing for me though."

By this time Edie was sobbing. "Amy, I'm so sorry. I don't know what to say. You are so strong. She got up and sat down on the couch with Amy and hugged her tightly."

"Do you remember how Mother always said, "You are what you think?" The paradox was she filled us o full of negativity, that she hijacked any constructive thoughts we might have. I used those very words to pull myself up. I told myself I was strong, and no one would ever pull me down again and it worked. Ironically, when I realized I was pregnant, I never suffered like you would think. Putting her up for adoption was never an option. All I could think of was my child was going to have all the love we never had and the opportunity to make her own choices. I still use those words every day. When I was raped, it took me a while to get back up again but I believe I'm even stronger for it. Then God gave me Amanda and it changed my life. I am here for you if you need me. I know Aaron hasn't been feeling well and you're worried about him."

"Oh Amy, you amaze me. After everything you've been through and you're worrying about me." She threw herself in her sister's arms; time seemed to stand still as they held each other, each drawing energy from the other.

***

Chapter Seventeen

Dr. Upshaw

True to her word, Edie made an appointment for Aaron with Dr. Upshaw, an internist, the following Monday. They had to start somewhere. Aaron admitted to Edie he hadn't been to a doctor except for Dr. Trent since he left Vietnam and agreed he needed a thorough check-up.

"Monday morning, Aaron and Edie were sitting in front of Dr. Upshaw's desk. His kind eyes reacted now and then as he listened intently as Aaron filled him in on his symptoms. Aaron told Dr. Upshaw he hadn't seen a doctor since he left the hospital in Vietnam except for Averton and Dr. Trent. Dr. Upshaw's countenance, his height of 5'4, and his shiny bald head gave you a feeling of confidence as did his crisp white coat. You just couldn't pinpoint exactly why. He reminded Aaron of a favorite uncle he had when he was a child. He knew Dr. Upshaw wouldn't read him stories like his Uncle Donald did, but he had a kind face and continued to listen intently to Edie as she gave him her perspective on how Aaron had been feeling.

"So, Aaron it looks like you were exposed to some pretty strong chemicals during your tour of duty."

"That's not what they told us. We were told not to worry. They said whatever residual toxins remained after they decimated the jungle and we flew into it, the constant monsoons we dealt with daily would take care of it. I did have asthma as a child."

"That doesn't surprise me, par for the course. Your breathing doesn't suggest asthma to me at all. I'm going to run a battery of tests today to see if we can get to the bottom of what we're dealing with." He smiled and it lit up the room. Aaron liked this doctor and knew if he had anything, Dr. Upshaw wouldn't rest until he found it. He could feel his breathing change as if the air had been let out of a balloon.

"So, honey what do you think?"

"It's too soon for me to decide yet. Dr. Upshaw did run an impressive amount of tests but I'm still tripping over finding you in a crumpled heap on the floor."

"I like him. He conjures up memories of a favorite uncle on my mother's side, whom I had as a child. Uncle Donald always smelled of Old Spice, coffee, and butterscotch candy and read to me sometimes."

"He's adorable but we'll see. What are you ordering? I think I'll have the Beef Wellington but first I need a glass of Cabernet Blanc. It will calm me down."

"Honey, you need to try not to worry. I bet all my symptoms can be traced back to the sleep deprivation I've been dealing with ever since my nightmares came back. Sleep deprivation is a big deal. They still use it on the POWs to get information from them, and it works," Changing the subject, he picked up the menu. "I think I'll have lemon trout almondine, a side salad, and a glass of white wine. I'll need to see their wine list."

Edie knew Aaron was in serious denial but maybe finding excuses for every symptom he had was the only way he could cope with his fear. It was comical how he had a different excuse for every symptom. If it helped him, she wasn't about to say anything until his test results came back.

Less than three weeks later they were back in Dr. Upshaw's office sitting in front of his desk.

"Aaron and Edie, thanks for coming in this morning. I've gone over your tests, specifically your X-rays, and cat scans and I'm afraid we've found a suspicious growth in your left lung. I'm going to recommend a specialist. Dr. Fairfield is a renowned oncologist and a colleague of mine, and he is the best. I would send anyone in my own family to him. Unfortunately, we can't be sure if it is malignant or not. We'll have to do a biopsy to find out. I'm convinced you're continual exposure to Agent Orange has played a major role in this. Do you smoke?"

"I did, but I've quit. I thought it might make a difference and I wouldn't be so out of breath.

"Good, don't start back up." Edie was mortified when she started to cry. What would Aaron think? She didn't want to let him know how worried she was but they both knew something wasn't right. Hearing it was like their whole world had taken on a horrible black cloud. Aaron was noticeably quiet.

Edie was so upset she told Aaron she just wanted to go home. Eating out was the last thing she wanted to do.

Aaron knew Edie was crying even though she was standing at the sink with her back to him wiping down an already spotless counter. Putting his hands on her shoulders, he turned her around, pulled her into his arms, and held her there without either of them speaking for a while. Putting his hand under her chin he made her look at him. "Honey, this doesn't have to be a death sentence you know. We don't know for sure if it's cancer yet and even if it is, I'm a fighter. You know, when I was in Vietnam, nothing made any sense to me. I couldn't deal with all the killing and seeing people I fought beside me dying every day. At times, I wanted to get that bullet with my name on it so it would be over. Then at Averton, I heard your sweet voice for the first time at the lowest point in my life. I didn't know it then, but it was like a ray of pure light pulling me out of all the pain. I fell in love with that voice before I even met you. I know the war screwed me up but falling in love with you has been the best thing that has ever happened to me. Because of you, I wanted to live again, even have a family one day. Do you think I would ever give that up without a fight?"

"Oh, Aaron, I love you so much," she said through her tears. It was then she saw his tears and put her head on his chest so he wouldn't realize she knew he was crying. They stood like that as if time didn't exist. All that mattered for the moment was the strength they could absorb from each other.

Time moved along at a pace that had become their new daily routine. They met Dr. Fairfield and after Aaron's biopsy, an agonizing seven days later it was confirmed that he indeed had stage four cancer in his left lung. Aaron took it head-on like the fighter he was. Dr. Fairfield's diagnosis shattered Edie and all of a sudden, she was faced with the biggest challenge of her life. Edie secretly vowed to stand beside him in the battle for his life; she would find the strength from somewhere. Aaron insisted that they should go on with their lives the best they could, and she should still sing. "Remember the butterflies, Edie," he said. Grab every minute you have baby, and I'll do the same." He never missed a day at work even though the chemotherapy made him so sick some days, he couldn't keep a glass of water down. He loved his students and being at the airfield was the medicine that kept him going.

***

"One day, Edie was home a day early from cutting her tour short. She hadn't been feeling well but was standing at the kitchen counter peeling potatoes and making a weak attempt at preparing dinner. Suddenly, she raced to the bathroom. Pushing the door open, she saw Aaron kneeling in front of the toilet too late. She only had time to turn to the sink and lose everything.

Aaron was immediately at her side, applying a damp washcloth to her face. "Honey, are you okay? You came home early because you were sick, didn't you? Do you think you've picked up a virus?"

"I don't know."

"Maybe it's "sympathetic nausea," At that Aaron started to laugh. I've heard of husbands doing that when their wives were pregnant but that would be ridiculous." His crazy sense of humor was infectious. By this time, they were both hysterical laughing with tears running down their faces when Edie suddenly stopped, remembering it had been two months since she had a period. There had been so much going on she'd never noticed.

"Dear God!"

Aaron looked at her as if he read her mind. "Could it be?" His face lit up like a Christmas tree.

"I'll make an appointment first thing in the morning." She said. Aaron was ecstatic, grinning like a kid, and twirling her around until he saw her pale face.

"Maybe this isn't the best idea in your condition." Beacon heard all the commotion and came charging into the bathroom, took one whiff, sneezed, turned around, and sprinted out the door, plowing into the door frame as he slid past them. They burst out laughing again and Aaron

121

convinced Edie to go lie down and he would finish cleaning the bathroom.

Dr. Fairfield, the Oncologist

"Edie, this is Barbara, Dr. Fairfield's nurse. Dr. Fairfield would like to schedule an appointment with both you and Mr. Weissman to go over Aaron's labs and X-rays. I have some dates for you if that will help?"

"Okay, I'll have to get back to you for next week. I'll need to get with my manager and do some rescheduling before I can commit. I'll call you Friday at the latest." Edie's hands were shaking; her heart was pounding so hard she felt like someone sucked all the air out of her lungs. She knew it was bad if Dr. Fairfield requested, they both be there. "How am I ever going to tell Aaron?" She said aloud.

"Tell me what?"

Edie was overcome with love and pain for Aaron as she looked at his beautiful face. "Dr. Fairfield's nurse called to schedule an appointment to go over your labs and X-rays. How does next week sound for you? Are you free?"

"That will take some juggling, but I'll manage. I need to go and find out if the chemo is working anyway. I feel lousy all the time. Maybe I'm anemic. I don't think I should be this tired."

Edie's head was spinning. Would she be able to get Travis to reschedule her Philadelphia tour? How could she be strong enough for Aaron if it were bad news when she felt like she had a knot in her throat already? "I hear you, honey. Let me know. I have to let her know no later than Friday, okay?"

"Sure, I will."

"Edie, why aren't you packing for your Philadelphia tour on Tuesday?"

"Travis called and it seems Karen, one of my backup singers has strep throat which throws all of us out of the water since it is so contagious. He had no choice but to reschedule. I thought we could go together on Monday or Tuesday morning and have a leisurely lunch at Tony's. You know how much you love his spaghetti and garlic bread."

"You mean like a date? Sounds great to me."

Dr. Fairfield was exactly what you might expect from an oncologist with twenty-five years of experience under his belt. At one time, he suffered with every one of his patients when he had to give them a cancer diagnosis and silently grieved when they eventually died. His wife Carrie kept telling him his job would kill him. At some point he became so jaded, that some people thought he was cold and indifferent. Sadly, his empathy had made him an old man at sixty. His stooped shoulders, complete baldness, and a slight tremor of his hands demonstrated what a toll his body had endured. Only God could see in his heart and know what he felt.

"Aaron, I appreciate you coming in this morning. Aaron, my team has gone over your X-rays and labs." Putting Aaron's X-ray on the screen, he said. "I'm so sorry to tell you the chemo is not working. As you can see the tumor is not shrinking and now you have a new growth in the right lung. Your labs are showing that you are anemic as well. This happens with chemo sometimes, unfortunately. This would account for you being so tired all the time. Additionally, your numbers confirm it is not working. My advice would be to stop the chemo."

"How long do I have?"

"Six months, maybe a little longer. If you have anything you want to do now, I suggest you make plans to do so. I would stop flying if you haven't already. I am so sorry."

Edie's vow to be stoic caved under the pressure and she slumped down in the chair crying softly. She couldn't believe it.

"Aaron, do you want to just go home? I could make us a sandwich." Dr. Fairfield stepped out of the room for a couple of minutes out of respect and to give them some privacy.

"Why would I do that? I was looking forward to our date tonight. Aren't you? Honey listen to me. We're all going to die someday. Only God knows our expiration date. Dr. Fairfield may think he knows mine. Who knows how much better I'll feel after I get off the chemo? I'm miserable and can't keep anything down. I'm rapidly losing my quality of life. Now's your chance to get me to go organic. Let's go get something to eat. All of a sudden, I'm starving.

Chapter Eighteen

Edie was completely overwhelmed. Aaron was still in denial. He was on a mission to eat healthily and frantically researching library information on how to turn his life around and initiate healing for his body. Edie decided to jump in with him. She didn't have much faith in it but if it was what he wanted, she was all for it. At first, she couldn't tell any difference.

"Aaron, how do you feel? If I didn't know better, I'd swear you had some color to your face."

"Believe it or not, I do feel better. I think my strength is coming back. At least I'm not puking my guts out."

"Aaron, do you think your continual exposure to Agent Orange caused your lung cancer?"

"I don't know. I always wondered. We were told no, it was harmless, but I had my doubts. You wouldn't believe how dense the jungles were in Vietnam. Our guys went in ahead of us on every mission and sprayed with Agent Orange to kill the dense foliage so we could see the enemy.

It was surreal to watch everything disintegrate in front of our eyes like some kind of crazy time-lapsed photography, and then we flew in right behind them."

"That's horrible. We need to let Dr. Fairfield know. You know how Dr. Upshaw feels already."

"At this point, what does it matter? The damage has already been done. Hopefully, I can regain my strength by eating right, taking better care of myself, and getting back some quality of life."

Edie wasn't so sure but didn't want to cause Aaron any more stress. She certainly was going to do some research on her own. In the meantime, she was going to give Aaron all the support she could in whatever he wanted to do. It was so wonderful to see him have some energy again and he sounded more like himself than he had in months. The first thing she needed to do when they got home was call Travis, her agent. She was going to have to do some juggling so she could get a couple of weeks off. He wasn't going to be happy about it. In his defense, it would put him in a bind, but she knew he would be there for her no matter what. He was more than a friend and treated her like a daughter.

Aaron was standing at the window enjoying the morning and imagining what flowers he wanted to plant if he continued to get his strength back when they found their dream home. He noticed Beacon playing with something. "Edie, what has Beacon got? It looks like a mouse or a small animal."

They both ran out the door and saw Beacon had a small kitten in his mouth. "Beacon, come here buddy." Beacon came trotting up to Aaron with the tiny kitten in his mouth. They had immediately bonded, and the kitten hung docilely from his mouth as if it were his mother holding him. Beacon, time to come in the house now, buddy. Beacon proudly carried his new friend gently into the house looking like a proud parent.

"Where do you suppose it came from? It's such a tiny little thing. I hope it's weaned because Beacon thinks it's his now." Beacon gently deposited the little guy on the nearby ottoman and the kitten immediately started meowing in a loud voice. Beacon gently picked it back up in his mouth and started carrying it again and walking around the house with it.

"I think you're right. Looks like we have a new member added to the Weissman family. I'll take it to the vet in the morning and see how old he is and if he has been weaned etc. He sure is tiny." Amy gave it a little saucer of evaporated milk and it drank like it was starving and got its whole body in the saucer to drink. When he was finished Edie had to wipe him down with warm water. Edie fixed a little box for him, and he went right to sleep. In the middle of the night when Edie got up to go to the bathroom, she went downstairs to check on him and the little box was empty. Following a hunch, she went back upstairs, and sure enough on the floor on Aaron's side of the bed Beacon and his new friend were sound asleep in Beacon's massive dog bed. The little guy was curled up tightly under Beacon's back leg.

Edie was trying not to get too excited. It had been eight months and Aaron was doing so well. He'd even put on some weight and had a full head of hair. He was back at work half days with his students again. He looked so good. She decided going on a tour would be against her better judgment, but Aaron insisted. "Aaron, are you sure you'll be okay? I have some unused vacation, you know."

"Absolutely. Beacon will take care of me like he always does." Beacon looked up at Aaron with adoring eyes as if he knew exactly what he was saying. We'll get Ms. Hayworth to come one day to clean while you're gone, and she can cook for us too. Beacon loves her or maybe it's her chuck roast he loves. It's only a week. If it will make you feel any better, you can bring a surprise back for Beacon and me. Sweetheart, I think I'm going to beat this. I can feel it," he said and rushed to answer the phone.

"Edie, you have a phone call. I think it's the hospital, honey."

"Ms. Carrington, this is Barrow Hospital. Your mother has been in an accident. She's asking for you. I'm her nurse. Please ask for Betty when you come to the front desk."

"An accident? Is she okay?"

"Aaron, my mother has been in an accident."

Edie looked at Aaron. "Edie just go. Do you want me to drive?"

"No, I'll call you when I get to the hospital."

Edie tried not to gasp when she saw her mother in the hospital bed through the hospital glass and how frail she was. She had a canula in her nose and an IV in her arm with a couple of bags of fluids feeding into her battered and bruised body. When they told her she was in an automobile accident Edie assumed she was a passenger with someone else. The doctor on duty told her she had been by herself on a road trip and was hit head-on by a drunk driver.

"But doctor, that's impossible. My mother doesn't drive."

"I'm sorry, Ms. Carrington, but she was certainly driving. I'm Dr. Manse by the way, and sorry to be the bearer of such bad news. I talked to the ambulance driver myself. I was the doctor on duty in the emergency room when they brought her in. I'm afraid we've done all we can. She had a lot of internal bleeding, a collapsed lung, a ruptured spleen, and one of her kidneys was beyond repair. We were able to stop the internal bleeding for now but, in my opinion, she wouldn't be able to survive the removal of her kidney. Given her age and current medical limitations, I don't think she'll make it through the night. She is drifting in and out and asking for you."

Edie lightly knocked on the open door to her mother's room. Nothing could have prepared Edie for seeing the tiny frail person lying in the fetal position in a hospital bed facing the window. Edie struggled with Dr. Manse's diagnosis and the finality of the prognosis. "Mother, it's Edie, I'm here."

Edie's hands were shaking so hard she gripped her handbag to keep from dropping it. It was all she could do to keep from turning around and bolting to her car as fast as her legs would carry her without making a scene. It had been at least a year since she had seen or spoken to her mother.

"Edie, is it really you?"

Olivia slowly rolled over, pressed the button on the railing, and elevated her frail body to a sitting position. When her mother opened her eyes, one eye was so swollen Edie could barely see any color through the tiny slit. Edie couldn't believe she thought she saw a tear running down her mother's cheek. She wasn't sure if her mother's eyes were watering from having been asleep or all the physical trauma from the accident.

"Please sit down. Let me look at you. It's been a long time, hasn't it? I guess I couldn't blame you if you never came. Edie, I'm so sorry for all the pain I've caused you. I know I made a lot of mistakes with you and Amy when you girls were growing up. Her voice was barely a whisper and Edie strained to hear her. I had no excuse as my parents, your grandparents you never got a chance to know, were very loving Godly people. I was the lead singer for a band when I was young and a big disappointment to my parents. You probably got your singing talent from me. Of course, getting married and having kids ended that."

"Mother, thank you. I didn't realize. You're right it was particularly rough for us. We were so young we didn't understand. I can't speak for Amy, but I forgive you."

"You have no idea what that means to me. I know Amy will never forgive me or come and see me, but do you think you might come by again and bring my grandchild when it's born? You must be so excited," she said, smiling at her baby bump. I would like to meet your husband. I read you got married in the paper. You were always such a good girl. When social services came to get you girls, I just sat on the stairs in shock for hours after they left. I can still hear your screams. I cried until I had no tears left. The worst part was I knew it was my fault and I'd have to live with it for the rest of my life. I didn't know for years that your father stuck you and Amy in foster care because he didn't have the backbone to stand up to Oovia. I am so sorry, Edie. I know you don't believe it, but I did love you and your sister, and always will. I think it's impossible to show love when you have never learned to love yourself. For whatever reason, I was always looking for that validation from others instead of drawing from my roots or the faith I had acquired so many years ago. I made the grave mistake of putting security before everything. If I had never married Edwin, you girls could have had a completely different life. I can't take back those years no matter how much I wish I could. I think it was harder for you than Amy. You were always so sensitive but look what you've accomplished for yourself. You are a famous singer. I love your music. You should be proud of yourself. I hope someday you'll be able to find closure with the past. Don't make the mistake of following in my footsteps. Embrace who you are Edie. You have a successful career despite everything. I don't know what made me the way I was with you girls. I came from a God-fearing and loving family. I know Amy hates me and I deserve it, but I hope she can find some peace for her sake one day." She reached for Edie's hand and drifted off. Edie sat with her mother the rest of the night and at 2:00 a.m. Olivia Carrington Martin quietly slipped away with a deathbed apology only a few hours before, still on her lips.

Edie barely remembered leaving the hospital and getting in her car or the ride home. Aaron met her at the door, took one look at her face, and took her in his arms. He walked her up the steps, took off her clothes, and helped her into a gown. She fell asleep immediately with her back against his chest and his arms wrapped around her. She was barely aware of him getting up until he came into the bedroom with two steaming cups of coffee. She couldn't believe it was morning. Propped up in the bed together and sipping their coffee, she was grateful Aaron didn't ask her any questions. That was how he was. They drank their coffee in silence. He knew instinctively she needed to process everything and would talk as soon as she could and he was confident, she knew he would be there when she needed him.

Chapter Nineteen

"Mr. Weissman, I'm Calvin Ainsworth. How are you?" he said extending his hand. I'd like to sign up for Merriweather Flight School if I could. I have a friend who studied under you and my dad or "Moose" as everyone called him, fought with you."

"Are you kidding me? I can't believe it. Of course, I remember your dad. How is he? Who is your friend? You have my undivided attention."

"Brent Skylar; he said if I went to flight school anywhere it had to be here. My dad got extremely ill after he came home. He eventually recovered but has recently been diagnosed with bladder cancer. I'm convinced his cancer is directly caused by his continual exposure to Agent Orange during his tour of duty in 'Nam."

"I am so sorry son. You need to give me your dad's number so I can look him up."

"Do you have any flight experience? How old are you?"

"I'm nineteen sir, and I'm afraid I'm starting from scratch. I've wanted to fly since I was a kid."

Calvin reminded Aaron of himself when he was young and on fire to learn everything he could about flying. Becoming a pilot meant everything to him for as long as he could remember. He liked this kid's energy, all 6'4" of his gangly frame. It seemed like only yesterday that he was this young and idealistic himself.

"Calvin, starting from scratch can be a plus. This way, you're not coming in with any preconceived ideas. My recommendation to you would be to attend our ground school first. I can give you all the written materials you will need for the weekend. I'm just starting a new class of eight and you can join them. We're also a registered testing facility so you'll be able to take your written exam at the end of your studies and have an idea of the principles you'll be learning in the rest of your flight training. It will be a grueling weekend I'm not going to lie to you. Some put their written exam off until the middle, but like I said it is my recommendation for the smoothest transition to the actual flying. You'll make your dad proud."

"No sir, I appreciate it. When do I start and where do I sign?"

***

Edie's tour was going well but it was getting harder and harder to focus on her music when she worried about Aaron and how he was feeling back home all the time. She loved singing so much and the adoration from her audience still took her breath away and thrilled her to the bone. Calling wasn't the same thing as being there. She knew he wouldn't tell her if everything wasn't okay over the phone anyway. She tired so much easier now because of the baby."

"Travis, you've been good to me over the years. You've believed in me from the beginning when I wasn't sure if I was going anywhere with my music. You've been like a

133

father to me but hear me out. I'm tired and it's getting harder and harder for me to keep up. The baby is taking all my energy. I'm taking off for maternity leave and please don't book any more tours for me now. I'll keep in touch. I need to take care of myself, and I've got a husband at home who needs me." She surprised herself and knew Travis was in shock. Well, he better get used to it. Aaron was first, her career second.

"Edie, I get it. We'll manage somehow. I know once you make up your mind, that's it anyway. Go, and be with Aaron as long as you can. Don't forget you can always come back, and I know you will at some point. It's in your blood.

She gave Travis a big hug and was still humming, *I am woman, hear me roar* when she picked up her purse and coat and headed for the door. She could feel Travis' eyes on the back of her head but that was okay. What was he going to do? She had made him a rich man over the years. She couldn't think any farther ahead than spending every precious minute they had left with Aaron.

The New House

"Edie come on. We can't be late. This is important. Good realtors don't grow on trees."

"I'm coming," she called from the bathroom. She wondered why she even bothered to dress. She looked like a bowling ball with arms and legs, was at the waddling stage, and felt like she'd been pregnant her whole life. They had looked at so many houses; this was important. It was exactly what they had been looking for and wanted one more walk-through before they told Tiffany Truite they were taking it. "Beacon, you, and Miso hold down the fort, okay?" She had to smile at the two as they were inseparable. They were the odd couple. Miso was growing like a weed, and it was hilarious to see them chase each other up and down the hall. Beacon was acting like a puppy. When she took Miso to Beacon's vet, he said other than a few fleas the kitten was healthy; just small from being undernourished, and had already been weaned from its mother. Its mother might have been killed and its siblings may not have been as lucky in finding a new home. It turned out Miso was a girl; of course, this made no difference at all to Beacon.

"Tiffany, what about schools? How far are we from the nearest grade school?" she asked, rubbing her huge tummy.

"You're only three blocks from Evergreen. It goes through the eighth grade. There is a high school not eight blocks away." She said smiling.

Aaron was in the kitchen with a tape measure taking window measurements in every room. Sweet Aaron; always planned and organized everything. He put her to shame in that department.

"What do you think Aaron?" she asked in a low voice. I'm ready. It's everything I've ever dreamed a home should

135

be. I love the big yard for our children. I'm sure Beacon will love it."

"Me too. Do you want me to make her an offer? I don't think we've overlooked anything, do you? We need to be sure before we decide."

"Let's do it. We don't need to think about it anymore." If it involved any kind of a major decision, Eddie and Aaron were exact opposites. At this rate, she'd be in labor before Aaron made up his mind.

Grabbing Edie, he spun her around and kissed her before he hurried off to find Tiffany and tell her the good news.

Things started moving pretty fast much to Edie and Aaron's delight. Tiffany, their realtor jumped at their offer, and they scrambled to schedule a closing date that would fit in with their schedules. Edie's due date was breathing down on them as well and they wanted to get into their new home before the baby came.

A week later their closing date was imminent, and Edie was busy canvassing some of the things she wanted to pack separately before the movers did their thing. She was in Aaron's chest of drawers and felt a velvet-covered box in the back of the second drawer. Pulling the box out and opening it she saw there were at least half a dozen or more medals in it. She wondered why Aaron never mentioned them to her. His parents would have been so proud if they were still alive. "Beacon did you know your daddy was a hero?" His friendly bark and rapid wagging of his tail implied he did. "Of course, you do, he tells you everything, doesn't he?" She laughed.

"Aaron, are you sure you're up to this wedding? Amy and Tom were getting married in only four weeks and Amy suggested having it at Edie and Aaron's new house because of Aaron's failing health. If he needed to lie down, it would be easier for him to do so. He was still working and, on the surface, looked great but Edie could see in his eyes when sudden exhaustion caught up with him and it was happening more often.

"Of course, this is important for everyone. What about you honey? You're so close to your due date and we haven't even moved yet? How are you going to manage? The wedding is only four weeks away.'

"You've got a point, but the movers are going to do the biggest part of it and Amy and Tom will be setting up. Amy has her dress already and she told me Tom has rented his tux. If the weather permits the wedding will take place outside in the garden and if not, we'll move it to the sunroom. It's a small wedding and we'll make it work. Amy is so happy. Are you going to wear your uniform since Tom has asked you to be his best man?"

"I wasn't planning on it, but Amy asked me if I would."

"I was going through things the other day to pre-pack before the movers got here and I found your medals in one of your dresser drawers. You never mentioned them. Your dad would have been so proud."

"I guess I have so many mixed feelings about them and so much guilt about Hank's death, I just put them where I wouldn't have to be reminded of them. I can't wrap my mind around being decorated for bravery when so many men are gone and died because of their bravery, and I survived." Edie ached for the pain in his voice.

The movers did an exceptional job of packing up everything and just as professionally unpacked and were happy to place the furniture wherever Edie indicated. Beacon was a little unnerved about all the changes but quickly adapted when he saw the enormous backyard and huge venerable oak tree that provided full shade for all the naps a dog could ever ask for.

The house was beautiful with its double wooden framed glass doors with side lights destined to forever have Beacon's and Miso's nose prints, and the house sat on a double lot. Aaron wanted to add some landscaping so was busy lining up a crew while Edie was racing back and forth to town trying to cover everything.

Getting everything done with Aaron's illness and Amy's wedding looming over their heads was challenging, to say the least. The movers had done a stellar job of unpacking and placing furniture where Amy told them, but she knew she would have to change it again at some point until she got it the way she wanted it. They both did the best they could and started making plans for Amy's wedding. Edie thought she must have been crazy to have agreed to have it at their house. She was just getting back from the salon after treating herself to a manicure, pedicure, and a rinse of her hair.

"Edie, you look beautiful, Aaron said, taking her in his arms. "Come, I want to show you something."

"What did you buy this time?" She could tell he was excited about something with a big grin from ear to ear and looking at her like a lovestruck puppy."

"Close your eyes and I'll show you." Edie closed her eyes and Aaron slowly led her from the kitchen with all the patience of Job, cautioning her to be careful as they exited from the back door, and down the two steps off the huge patio and into the massive backyard." Finally, when she felt they had walked the whole patio and yard, he carefully positioned her body the exact way he wanted and said, "Okay, you can open your eyes now. Edie gasped. The backyard looked like something straight out of Better Homes and Gardens. The landscapers under his supervision had stationed a rose arbor strategically in the yard with a white iron bench under it so you could sit and enjoy everything from different angles. Young rose bushes had been planted on either side, but it was too soon for them to proudly exhibit too many of their colors yet. There were fruit trees strategically planted framing the back of the fence. What took her breath away was the triangular-shaped garden in the back corner of the chain link fence. It was filled with mostly fuchsia clusters of lantana and there were butterflies everywhere. On the decorative bricks that framed the garden sat a small statue of a cherub with blond curls and a butterfly sitting on her chubby shoulder. Of course, just as she saw it Beacon had managed to deter one in flight and was busy chasing it until it flew away."

"It's a butterfly garden, isn't it? You made me a butterfly garden. Oh, Aaron, she said throwing her arms around him with tears in her eyes. I love you so much."

"I take it this means you like it?" He was grinning from ear to ear like the proverbial Cheshire cat.

Chapter Twenty

The weather provided a perfect backdrop for Amy and Tom's wedding ceremony. Amy was breathtaking in a pale peach floor-length gown with her luxurious blond hair pulled up and baby's breath woven throughout her curls. She carried a bouquet of tiny silk peach and white miniature roses. Edie was her maid of honor in a lovely two-piece beige maternity suit and low sling strap heels of the same color. Aaron in full dress uniform complete with medals, walked Amy down the short aisle of guests to Tom who stood waiting under the arbor so beautifully decorated with temporary artificial peach roses that matched the bride's dress. Amanda was glowing as the adorable flower girl proudly dropped a trail of peach rose petals and captured the heart of everyone as she walked down the aisle. Beacon always ready for a job, was the ring bearer who captivated everyone with his peach bow tie and the lovely, decorated basket with its regal peach pillow holding the rings that he carried by the handle in his mouth so carefully. After the ceremony, everyone joined the bride and groom on the decorated patio with a beautiful ice sculpture of Rodin's, *The Kiss.* In the back of the massive patio, several long tables had been set up with food for the guests, under a generous-sized tent in case of inclement weather. It couldn't have been more romantic when the guests were able to dance the night away under the stars on the front section of the patio. Edie couldn't believe they had pulled it off without a hitch. "Aaron, you look tired," Edie said. I'm sure everyone would understand if you snuck off and lay down for a bit."

"No way, I'm enjoying dancing with my beautiful wife. If anyone needs to take a break, it should be you." As they passed the food tent, they both saw Beacon, still with his bow tie. At the same time, Miso had stretched out his full length under one of the tables and was out cold in the well of Beacon's hip. "It looks like it was a big day for everyone." He chuckled.

The following week, Edie had just poured Aaron and herself a cup of coffee when she got a pain and stopped for a minute, putting the cups down on the counter. It passed in a couple of minutes, so she decided it couldn't be labor yet and headed for the stairs. Her body was probably reacting to all the extra work.

"Thank you, honey. I should be waiting on you and bringing you coffee. How are you feeling?"

"Like I've been pregnant my whole life." She waddled to the side of the bed, backed up to it, pulled herself up and back as far as she could manage, and stared at her swollen feet.

"You are getting close to your due date, aren't you?"

"It's here, baby." No sooner were the words out of her mouth than she got another pain; this one sharp.

Aaron sat straight up, almost dropping his coffee cup as he put it on the nightstand so hard coffee splashed over the top, jumped out of bed, and accidentally stepped on Beacon's tail in the process. Beacon yipped, scrambled to his feet, and took off highly insulted. Aaron was immediately at Edie's side. "Shouldn't you call the doctor? I'm worried."

"It's probably false labor. Let's just wait a bit. Can you believe I have to pee again?" She struggled to get up and when she did her water broke and hit the carpet like someone dropped a water balloon.

"Dear God! "Edie, what do you want me to do?" He jumped up and raced through the bedroom door and took the stairs two at a time.

Edie managed to get to the landing, wet pants, and all. "Aaron, where are you going? she called down to him. She didn't get an answer and then heard the car running.

"Tell me it isn't so." Beacon came up to her, licked her hand, and whimpered. "Beacon, go get your daddy." At that, Beacon relieved to have a job, took to the stairs, gaining enough momentum that when he got to the bottom, he couldn't stop and slid into the door just as Aaron opened it.

Edie was shaking with laughter when they both came bounding back up the stairs. "Did you forget something? Help me to get to the bathroom. Then get my suitcase out of the bedroom, put it in the car, turn the engine off, and don't forget to put some food and water out for Beacon and Miso. I need to clean up."

By the time Edie got cleaned up and changed she was in full labor. Aaron helped her into the car and neither of them said much. She was surprised at how much pain she was in. Aaron was pale and focused on driving and Edie prayed he wouldn't get stopped for speeding. As soon as he pulled up to the door of the hospital, someone helped her into a wheelchair and put his hand on Aaron's shoulder, "Sir, you will have to move your car into the parking lot now. You're blocking the entrance. We will take your wife to the back and let you know where she is when you get back. You'll be able to sit in the waiting room until we come and get you,"

"Come with me, Mr. Weissman, your wife, and baby girl are doing fine. Mr. Weissman. Oh, for heaven's sake, nurse, bring me something, STAT. This joker has hit the floor. I knew I should have been a dentist like my dad."

Mr. Weissman, are you okay? Come on, man. You're a father now. Pull yourself together. Can you stand? Okay, sit here a minute," the male nurse said pushing a wheelchair under him. "Let me know when you get your land legs, and I'll take you back."

"I'm ready, Let's go."

"Aaron saw her as soon as they walked up to the viewing window of the nursery. She was tiny but so beautiful. He was so overcome with emotion he was afraid to speak and blow his cover. Passing out was one thing but tears were unacceptable. He was a dad. He couldn't believe it. "Edie, she's beautiful. She has your eyes. Of course, they're blue but I bet they're going to turn green soon. He couldn't believe how beautiful Edie looked with the baby in her arms, like being a mother was what she was born to do.

"What are we going to name her?'"

"How does Brittany Elizabeth Weissman sound?"

"I like it. It sounds strangely familiar, even though I don't think I remember any Brittany's in my life." He winked at her.

Edie and Aaron settled into being parents as naturally as if they had been doing it all their lives. Brittany was a good baby and adjusted to her days and nights like a pro to the delight of her parents. Aaron was in the nursery giving Brittany her morning bottle when the doorbell rang. "I'll get it." Edie hollered up. Beacon took to the steps two at a time to make sure he wasn't missing anything.

"May I help you?" The young man standing in their doorway was very tall, had a wonderful smile, and was dressed as if he had just come from the gym. He was wearing a prosthetic leg from the knee down.

"Yes, I'm looking for Aaron Weismann, a buddy of mine. We served in 'Nam together. Ted Allan," he said reaching out to shake her hand.

"What a wonderful surprise. He'll be thrilled. Come have a seat. I'll go get him. He's giving the baby a bottle."

"The baby, man do we have a lot to catch up on."

Edie ran upstairs to get Aaron with Beacon just coming down again, turning around, and escorting Edie back up the stairs.

Aaron was just putting Brittany down as she fell asleep before she could finish her bottle.

"Aaron, honey there's someone to see you."

"Oh no, I don't feel like seeing anyone honey. I was hoping to go lie down for about an hour. Is there anything you could do to get rid of them?"

"I'm sorry. I already told him you were feeding the baby."

Aaron was behind Edie on the steps, so he didn't see Ted at first until they got to the bottom of the steps, and he stood up from the chair he was sitting in.

"Dear God! Ted Allan, I don't believe it, man. How in the world did you find me?" he said. Running up to him he grabbed his friend and gave him a big bear hug.

Ted sat back down in the chair and Aaron sat in the inviting recliner next to him facing the silent massive television console. Beacon settled at his feet as always.

"Well, you remember Smitty?" He got the bullet with his name on it two days before the last day of his tour assignment. We lost four others that day, Tank, Gavin, and Scout. I lost my leg. I hear Moose has bladder cancer and it's terminal. I'm sorry man, he said when he noticed the pain on Aaron's face. Captain Van was writing the families and I caught him in a vulnerable moment I guess, and I wormed your last known address or Averton out of him. It was pretty easy after that. I was blown away that he gave it to me. He took the hit and loss of his men hard. He had some tough shoes to fill when you left but he turned out to be a good captain.

"Captain Van was devastated when he heard you were blind. We all were and of course, losing Hank was a big blow to the whole platoon. Captain Van was the one who had to notify his parents. But you're not blind now, buddy. I can't wait to hear that story. You know when I saw my leg lying on the ground blown to smithereens, I didn't want to live. I thought of Hank. He died a hero and didn't have to deal with any of the fallout. I didn't think Whitney would ever look at me the same way. Of course, it was all in my mind. My pity party almost cost us our marriage. I finally got it together and life is good. We're expecting our first child in the fall. The only effect it had on my manhood was in my mind and that was only for a short time."

Edie left to go to the kitchen and make some coffee and see if there were any of Ms. Hayworth's wonderful scones left. She could hear the excitement and emotion in their voices floating up from the living room. This was going to be so good for Aaron.

"You know I have lung cancer."

"Oh man, I am so sorry. I had no idea. Do you think it's from Agent Orange?"

"Yes, I do but I doubt if they'll ever admit it, at least in our lifetime. Don't feel sad for me for one minute, man. I am married to my soulmate, have a beautiful baby girl, and able to do what I love. I've already outlived my doctor's expiration date. In the words of Woody Allen, 'I'm not afraid of death. I just don't want to be there when it happens.' I don't want to leave my girls, but I'll be ready when the time comes."

"I'm happy for you man. In our world, we have to live one day at a time. You know that. I'm so thankful I got my head on straight, or I would have ruined my marriage. We are the ones that came back and what we make of the time we have left is what's important."

"Exactly, I'm so glad you found me, Ted. It's been like a lifeline for me. I needed to be reminded of how ultimately what we do with our lives is our responsibility. I see some of the unlucky ones in downtown Atlanta stoned and passed out in alleys any given morning while the rest of the world is safe at home in their beds."

***

"Aaron, it is so good to see you. How are you? It has been a while, hasn't it? Beacon, you're looking quite handsome today. I like your outfit." Dr. Faraday said, shaking his paw. Beacon was wearing a camouflage scarf around his neck and was the picture of content.

"Better than you would expect, I think. You know, I have lung cancer."

"No, I'm sorry to hear that, Aaron. I had no idea." Dr. Faraday tried to hide his shock. He did notice the minute Aaron walked in how much weight he had lost and how pale he was.

"It's okay. Believe it or not, I can certainly see God in this. When I saw Hank killed right in front of me, I was furious and couldn't justify all the killing and guilt that threatened to destroy me and my faith. I even prayed at one time to get that bullet that had my name on it so I could escape all the pain. I don't know when it happened but now, I realize God used the war and my temporary blindness to carry me to Averton. He knew the horrible feelings of isolation and loneliness I lived with every day, and he brought me straight to Edie. If I had got the bullet with my name on it like I wanted I never would have met Edie, fallen in love, got married, or had a baby girl.

We've bought our dream home, and now I am a flight instructor. I managed to finish school and secure an engineering degree. My parents would be incredulous since they wanted me to be a doctor, but I love it; flying is in my blood. One of my buddies, Ted Allan from 'Nam managed to track me down recently. It was so great to find out what had happened to my friends. I guess you would categorize it as closure. I've already exceeded the six months the doctors gave me. I don't know how long I have but what I do know is I'm going to continue to pack in as much living as I can with what time I do have until God decides to take me home."

"You amaze me, Aaron. Your sense of peace is something beautiful to behold and one for the books in my world. I'm so proud of you." He uncharacteristically gave him a fatherly hug.

"Thanks, Doc. No offense but this will be my last visit. I've got a lot of living to do yet and will be pretty busy."

"I completely understand. I'll miss you and Beacon a great deal."

***

Chapter Twenty-One

"Edie, how are you? It's been a while, hasn't it?"

"Yes, it has, and I apologize for not following up sooner, Dr. Kensing."

"Well, you're here now and that's what's important. Staying busy with your career, I imagine?"

"Off and on. Aaron has been ill. He has stage four lung cancer and is fighting the battle of his life. He is so brave. We have a little girl now, Brittany Elizabeth, and that keeps us both busy. Despite everything Aaron has insisted we live our lives and we have moved into our dream home."

"Wow, that's a lot. You certainly have your hands full. What would you like to talk about today?"

Coping, I guess, and making Aaron as happy as I can with the time we have left," she said tears running down her face. "He seems to be at peace and handling it better than I.

"Edie, death is something none of us can escape, you realize, but facing death so young is unbearable. I can only imagine what you must be going through. I am so sorry."

"You sound like Aaron. I wish I had his strength."

"Wait a minute, you have amazing strength and resilience. Most people would be bouncing off the walls having walked in your shoes. Grieving is not a sign of weakness; it is a necessary form of coping we all have to face at some time in our lives."

"I know you're right. My mother died in a car accident a couple of months ago. It's strange but when I was a child, I was always terrified of losing her. I had more than my share of nightmares about it. I did survive better than I ever imagined I would. I guess I have grown since then. Aaron always said we would heal each other with the love we had for each other."

"That is a profound observation on your part Amy. I'm immensely proud of you. Try to give yourself some space as far as your grief goes. I think you are doing amazing considering what you have on your plate right now. I hope you will continue to touch base with me if you can. Don't overlook the need for rest. You are dealing with a lot, and you must take care of yourself. Are you still touring?"

"No, I have taken a leave for a while so I can be with Aaron as long as I can. Thank you, Dr. Kensing for everything. I will. I promise."

"Honey, do you have any idea where my jacket is? I'm going to take Brittany and Beacon to the park. Come on, Beacon, be patient." Beacon was ready with his leash in tow and sitting up straight as a ramrod with his perfect posture making sure he didn't get overlooked.

"Are you sure Aaron? Are you up to it?"

"Of course, I am. Beacon will watch over me like he always does," Beacon had a small red plastic pouch attached to his harness with a note listing a name and number and saying, "Call in case of a medical emergency."

Grabbing a lunch, he'd made from the refrigerator that morning, putting it in the diaper bag and some treats for Beacon, he pushed Brittany in the stroller to the front door with Beacon following politely behind. "Don't worry, we'll be home in a few hours. The fresh air will be good for all of us." Loading up was hilarious as Beacon was determined to help and Brittany was transfixed watching her beloved Beacon trying to take the car seat belt in his teeth as Aaron attempted to strap her in.

When they got to the park, Brittany was still wide awake and fascinated with the view from her window. By the time she was back in her stroller, she was waving her hands and kicking her feet and of course, Beacon was beyond containing himself and started running in circles around Brittany's stroller. This launched Brittany into a fit of laughter, which only added fuel to the fire. The more Brittany giggled the sillier Beacon got. They fed off each other.

"Look, Brittany, at the pretty butterfly. A beautiful Monarch butterfly landed on Brittany's foot. When she reached for it, it flew off and Beacon started chasing it and when it flew above him, he lunged and plowed into a nearby bench letting out a yip. "Daddy loves butterflies. They are special and good luck. Did you know when you see one, someone has a message from heaven to deliver to their loved one?" Brittany squealed with excitement when the monarch circled back toward them and then flew away.

"Hi honey, how was the park?" Edie heard the car drive up but deliberately stayed in the kitchen as it was important these days for Aaron to feel as independent as possible even though they both knew he was getting worse. "I see the children had a good time." Brittany hung like a rag doll in her father's arms and Beacon hobbled to his downstairs bed in the living room and flopped down, sighed, and closed his eyes. She noticed the dark circles under Aaron's eyes immediately but was careful not to comment.

"It was wonderful. I don't know who fell more, Brittany or Beacon. They were busy chasing a butterfly."

"That's hilarious. I sure hope Brittany's not going to be a klutz like her father."

"God has that covered. Brittany's knee cartilage will not develop into bone until she is ready to start school."

"Really?"

"Fascinating, isn't it? The cartilage will start developing into bone in the center of her knee when she's about two and continue slowly until she is six. We can thank OU and my earlier days as a medical student for that bit of trivia."

"He sure does have it covered. She has a lot of tumbles ahead of her between now and when she starts school. I'm glad you had a good time honey." she said, reaching to put her arms around his neck.

Time, the Biggest Thief of All

"Edie could hear Beacon barking before she even got to the front door. He sounded frantic. She dropped the bags of groceries on the driveway and ran to open the door. Beacon flew out in front of her and was barking frantically, jumping up, then running ahead and circling back to see if she was following him. Edie followed Beacon to their bedroom and Aaron was lying on the floor face down. When she turned him over, he was unconscious, and blood was all around his mouth as if he had bitten his tongue. She ran to call an ambulance and suddenly heard Brittany crying. She ran to the nursery with poor Beacon on her heels. With Brittany in her arms, she raced back to the bedroom and lay Brittany on the bed. Aaron was semiconscious by this time, and she whispered to him he would be okay, and help was on the way. She was able to get their nanny on the phone. Fortunately, she lived less than a block away and showed up at the same time the ambulance did.

"Honey, I'm going to be right behind you and I'll see you soon." Edie didn't know if Aaron understood anything she was saying but she had to try anyway. When they shut the doors to the ambulance, the tears came so fast and furious, she had to sit in the car until she could pull herself together enough to drive.

When she got to the hospital, he was already in the emergency room, had been given oxygen, and a doctor was examining him.

"Mrs. Weissman, I'm Doctor Henley. I was only able to get some of his medical history from the file we have here on Mr. Weissman. I called your husband's doctor, and he's filled me in. He is cyanotic but we are giving him two liters of oxygen and that should help. I'm afraid the blood around his mouth may be coming from his lungs. Was there a lot of blood on the floor where he passed out? Is he currently receiving oxygen? Do you know how long he had been on the floor passed out?"

"I don't know how long he was out. I was gone for two hours at the supermarket. He seemed fine when I left. Yes, he takes oxygen at night. What do you think is going on?"

"I don't know yet, but we need to run some tests and find out. You know he has stage four lung cancer, and it appears to be in its final stages. If I were to guess, I would say he is seriously anemic from the chemo, but I won't know for sure until I can get the results of his blood work."

"He quit his chemotherapy months ago. He said he wanted to have some quality of life with the time he had left. There was no blood on the carpet where he was lying." Edie immediately began to cry. Dr. Henley looked disgusted and like he wanted to bolt and run.

"Alright then, you may go in and talk to him; he's awake. Sit with him if you like until the X-ray technician comes and gets him. He doesn't appear to be actively bleeding. He may have injured himself in some way when he fell."

Edie didn't have anything against Dr. Henley, but she didn't care for his bedside manner if he even had any at all. It was as if he just went through the motions and all the emotional makeup that makes us human was missing. Maybe, working in a hospital and around sick people did that to a doctor eventually. She was glad Aaron had good doctors because this one would have never been her choice.

"Aaron, how do you feel, honey? Do you remember what happened?"

"Is Brittany all right? I just put her down for a nap and was going to catch a little nap myself while she slept. I know I made it to the bedroom, but I don't remember anything after that."

"Brittany is fine. She's with Nelda. You passed out on the bedroom floor."

"Mr. Weissman, I'm glad you're awake. I'm Dr. Henley. My team has gone over your bloodwork and X-rays. I'm afraid the cancer has become more aggressive and is now in one of your kidneys. We will need to keep you for a few days and start your chemotherapy again. It may be necessary to surgically remove the affected kidney. You are anemic as well and could use some units of blood."

"Hold on, Dr. Henley, I don't want any more chemo or blood. I want to go home. I think it's obvious at this point there's nothing more you can do. I don't want to spend what time I have left on the toilet with my head over the wastebasket puking my guts out."

"You do realize it might buy you a little more time?"

"I do, but what good is more time if I have no quality of life? I choose to spend what time I have left with my family. I trust you will get my paperwork together so we can check out."

"Of course. I understand." At that, he headed for the door.

Edie thought it was too bad that his words were completely out of touch with his demeanor. He just wasn't capable of passing empathy onto his patients if he ever had any.

Making Aaron as comfortable as possible was a challenge but one Ms. Hayworth met head-on. She turned out to be a Godsend as she suggested increasing her household responsibilities. She was especially fond of both Edie and Aaron. They were able to use the oxygen company Dr. Henley recommended and needed it around the clock. They rented a hospital bed and put it into the living room. Beacon never left his station on the floor by Aaron's bed except to eat and go outside when nature called. Even Miso couldn't cheer him up. Edie hired a nurse to come in twice a day to bathe him and keep in contact with his doctor and anything else he might need. Aaron did agree to a couple of units of blood and a glucose IV. He had to admit he felt better. At night he insisted on sleeping in their bed so everything he needed was transferred to their bedroom. Poor Beacon went everywhere his beloved Aaron went. Edie could hear him padding down the stairs at night exiting through the pet door to take care of business and then racing back up the stairs to lay at Aaron's feet. Aaron's frame of mind changed immediately as soon as he got home. It broke her heart to see how much weight he had lost. Despite everything he seemed so happy to be home with everyone. They spent every minute together and while he slept, Edie started working on a song to keep her mind occupied. He slept a lot. At first, Edie couldn't put her finger on it but there was peace around him. She envied his sense of peace and struggled every day. With Beacon asleep at their feet one morning in the living room, and the baby asleep in her crib, Edie got on the couch with Aaron, snuggled up to him, laying her head on his chest. "Honey, how do you feel? Can I get you anything?"

"I think I have everything I need. Our little girl is sleeping in the other room, Beacon is snoring at our feet, and cuddling with the love of my life is all a man could ask for. I love you so much, Edie. You know, I feel surprisingly better this morning probably because of the units of blood and the glucose IV but let's not kid ourselves, honey, we need to start making plans."

Edie raised her head from Aaron's chest with tears running down her face. "I don't want to go there yet. I'm not ready. We have time."

"Honey, we have to talk about you and Brittany when I'm gone. It's an inescapable reality," Aaron said, holding her and rocking her. I want you to go on singing and writing your music. Write a song about our love. It's bound to fly off the charts. He smiled. It is the very core of who you are, and it will help you heal. We are more fortunate than most people financially so take Brittany to see Paris one day and experience the beauty of it, do everything you can; live your life with passion, honey. You only get one time around. Remember the butterflies. I have no regrets. You have made me so happy. I would give anything to have longer with you, but we both know God has another plan."

"I'll try, but God could still choose to heal you of your cancer. Don't you believe in miracles anymore?" She put her head down again on his chest so he wouldn't see she was still crying. He rubbed her back ever so gently.

"Of course, I do, honey. Can't you see the healing he has brought into our life already? He brought us together. Your heart has healed from your past. That was a prayer He answered for me. I can't remember the last time I had a nightmare. What about Brittany? She is truly a miracle, a manifestation of our love. He delivered Ted to our front door, and I was able to find out what happened to all my comrades. It depends on how you look at it. We are part of God's plan. I would love to stay and be with you and walk Brittany down the aisle one day but that is not part of his plan, but I trust it will be something wonderful. I'm ready to go home, Edie. I don't want to fight any more for every breath and I am so tired of the pain. I only hope God can forgive me for all the killing. I'm sad for the road ahead you face but I know in my heart you're going to be okay. When the time is right if you meet someone, follow your heart, and live with passion. You're too loving a woman to be alone the rest of your life. Share that capacity for love with another soul. It's your greatest gift. We'll be together again one day."

They held hands and were silent for what seemed an eternity before Edie said. "Aaron, you don't have to stay for me. When you're ready, you can go. You're right, I will be okay." It was the hardest thing she had ever done but she knew it was the one thing that could give him peace and the last thing she could do for him. Once again, he held her as she put her head on his chest, and she could feel his tears on her back through her blouse.

Chapter Twenty-Two

The next morning started like so many others. Edie rescheduled a hair appointment so she could bake some muffins and spend the day with Aaron. She hoped Aaron's appetite would improve since he was feeling a little better yesterday. She was going to make all his favorites for breakfast. The smells were driving Beacon crazy. When she finished, she put everything on a tray and started for the stairs. Beacon flew past her taking the steps two and three at a time. "Beacon, slow down." When she walked through the doorway, the first thing she saw was Beacon lying across Aaron. "Beacon, for God's sake what are you-----? She dropped the tray on the floor and ran to the bed. She knew Aaron was gone immediately. He looked like he was asleep; he had such a peaceful look on his face. She lay on the bed holding him and Beacon until she heard Brittany crying. Getting up, she told Beacon, "I'll be right back. Take care of Daddy for me."

Edie got through the next week in a daze. Only God himself knew how hard it was and he held her upright and allowed her to function somehow. Beacon was grieving and wouldn't leave their bedroom except to go to the bathroom and would barely eat. She allowed him to sleep on Aaron's side of the bed. She just didn't have the heart to do otherwise. Amy and Tom were at her side and helped make all the arrangements. She made sure Aaron had a full military funeral with honors. She knew it would mean a lot to him. It was the last thing she was able to do for him. She never realized how many people loved and appreciated Aaron. All his students from Meriweather Flight School attended the services. Caleb Rushing and Tom Prentiss, his college friends were there. Aaron had been so ill they hardly went anywhere but to the doctor or hospital for months, so she was surprised at how many of their friends were there. Ted Allen, and Captain Dan, his CO from Vietnam were there. Ted told her that Moose, his buddy from the war had just recently succumbed to bladder cancer and said they were probably together now exchanging old war stories. Edie knew he would have been so touched by the loyalty of so many. She hoped he approved of his funeral arrangements. She was thankful she was able to give him a military funeral with all the honors. He had a twenty-one-gun salute and the playing of taps. Each time a gun went off it felt like it took a piece of her soul. She decided to save his medals for Brittany since he told her how he felt and only wore them for Amy and Tom's wedding. When they handed her the folded flag his casket was draped in, her heart felt as if it was breaking. As they were leaving the cemetery and walking to the limousine, she was physically and mentally exhausted and didn't even try to contain the silent tears that would not stop running down her face when she heard Brittany giggle and felt her pull from her hand. She turned around just in time to see Brittany reaching for a beautiful brilliant teil-colored butterfly with black spots, on her dress as it flew off, circled back, and lit on her shoulder. She chuckled with delight and said, "Mommy, look!" Edie was mesmerized and stood and watched it for what felt like forever before it flew off. Brittany toddled after it, but it had accomplished its mission and disappeared as quickly as it came. Amy was behind her and was spellbound as well. "Looks like Aaron found a way to let you know he's okay, Sis. He loves you so much," she said, wiping her eyes with a well-soaked tissue. Afterward, Amy had arranged everything so their family and friends could come to the house. The food was tasteful and perfect for the occasion.

"Dear God, spare me, Caleb, please. Edie was laughing so hard tears were running down her cheeks. She had never heard the story of Aaron rescuing Caleb from sleeping off their partying in the big planter full of peonies in front of their dorm. They were furious with Tom the next day when they discovered he had beaten them to the dorm hours before and slept through everything.

"Edie, I'm Dr. Faraday, Aaron's psychiatrist. I'm not sure when it will serve as a comfort to you or expedite your healing, but I have to say in all my years of practice I have never witnessed a patient more in love. It has been a privilege to watch Aaron's transformation. It has been the love between you and Aaron and his unshakable faith that has healed his soul and enabled him to complete his journey. I doubt it was what either of you wanted but his courage didn't end on the battlefield, and I will never look at things the same since knowing him."

Whatever Edie did in the months after Aaron's funeral challenged her to the core, but she knew she needed to make a life for her and Brittany. There was so much that she had to do. Her mother had been gone for months but

159

Aaron's last days and funeral had taken priority. Edie and Amy were surprised that their mother's final wish was to donate her body to science, and it took a great deal of pressure off them. They finally started the monumental task of emptying their mother's house. Olivia Carrington Martin had left her entire estate to be divided between the two girls. Amy was surprised since she had only recently forgiven her mother and hadn't seen her in years. Losing Aaron and the funeral wasn't the only thing that had her stomach upset. Edie didn't have a clue what to do with her mother's house.

"Edie, first things first. I know it's overwhelming but let's just go through Mother's things, pack up what we might want, and donate the rest. The first thing we can do is get rid of that hideous chair in the living room she never let anyone sit on. They both giggled. We have plenty of time. We can rent her house until we decide if we want to sell it or not."

"Okay, that makes sense to me." Edie was emptying her mother's purse. Seeing all the cash her mother had in her wallet didn't begin to surprise her as much as seeing she had a current driver's license.

"Amy, how long do you think mother was driving, and why did she keep it such a secret? I know she was terrified to get behind the wheel of a car when we were kids, so she wouldn't let us drive?"

"I don't know. Maybe she only started driving after Edwin died and had no way to get around. I'm sure we'll never know now. How sad that she was able to emotionally keep us cripples for so many years."

"Edie, come here. You've got to see this." Amy was sitting on the floor Indian style in her mother's office with a huge scrapbook in her lap and another small stack of boxes open on the floor.

"What is all this?"

"Looks like Mother kept a scrapbook on your entire career starting from day one. I bet she has every clipping and article ever written about you. This is years of following you your whole life. I had no idea. Maybe the reason she was so hard on you was because she was the proudest of your continued success. She always talked about how we interrupted her chance to be a singer. Maybe she was living her dream vicariously through you. I can't believe it but there's even a scrapbook on me, my graduation from college, Amanda's birth announcement, my engagement announcement to Tom, and even our marriage and pictures from the Sunday section. Wait, here's one of those crazy metal boxes she always kept. She kept everything. Here's a receipt for a driver's course. Bingo. It's dated less than a week after Edwin died. I wonder why she never told us. If these things were important to her, why was she so lacking as a parent? We could have had such a different life. I just don't get it."

"I'm not sure she knew how. She did apologize on her deathbed. We have to give it to God. It's the only way we'll ever have peace. Don't cry, Sis. We can't go back but we can be better parents to Amanda and Brittany, and they'll always know they're loved because of it."

***

Out of the blue, Edie decided she had one more person she had to visit.

"Edie, is it really you and who is this adorable little girl with you?"

Edie couldn't believe the change in Diane Crain. She only recognized her previous foster mom by her soft voice and sweet smile. Exhaustion from so many years of taking care of other people's children had taken a toll on her now frail body. She was rail thin, and her hair was completely grey, but her beautiful brown eyes were exactly as she remembered them. They always made Edie think of a sweet doe. Her home that the girls spent three years in looked the same except for the haunting silence that held no children. It was immaculate, and everything was in its place as always. Edie looked over at the fireplace and all the pictures of so many children on the mantle. Mr. Crain's big recliner sat where it always did. She could visualize the little ones on the arms of his chair and at his feet as he read to them at bedtime.

"Where's Mr. Crain?"

"I lost him about five years ago. He was such a good man. He was pretty sick for years. He fought the fight, but cancer won. After he was gone, I stopped taking in children. It just wasn't the same after he died. Bobbie finished college, married a beautiful girl, and has a dental practice in Atlanta. They never had any children of their own. Ironic, isn't it? I knew we couldn't have children but always thought I would have grandchildren. You know Bobbie was a baby when he came to live with us. His mother died shortly after, and we adopted him and raised him as our own. I guess God had other plans."

"I had no idea. It would seem you were an important part of God's plan from the beginning. Look how many children's lives you've touched over the years. No telling what rewards He has planned for you in heaven. I know how much influence you had on me and Amy. I'm so sorry about Mr. Crain; he was a sweet man. I lost my husband this year. It has been difficult, but Brittany and I are doing the best we can. He was my soulmate and endured so much from Vietnam. I'll always believe our love healed each of us. I couldn't have made it without my music. I promised Aaron I would continue singing. He knew how much I loved it."

"I'm so glad you did. I have followed you for years. I love your music and am so proud of you Edie. I always knew you were special as I told you the day you girls left to go back to your mother and stepfather. I didn't know what you would encounter in your young lives, but I knew nothing would stop you until you found your dream. It looks like I was right."

When Diane held out her arms, it was all Amy needed as she rushed to them and hugged her. The tears flowed freely but it was therapeutic for both of them, and they both promised to see one another again soon. Diane watched out the living room window as Edie helped Brittany down the steep walkway to Edie's car parked at the foot of the hill. Diane knew it was probably going to be the last time she would see Edie. She was born with a heart problem but managed to live a full life despite it but after being forced into an early retirement, it had caught up with her. In her mind, the loneliness was going to kill her before her heart did. She missed the children. She couldn't keep any weight on no matter what she did. Her doctors told her she had kidney disease and gave her less than a year. She was at peace and Edie's visit had given her a wonderful gift. Few of us are fortunate enough to receive confirmation that we chose the right path in life. Edie was a walking testament to Diane's choice and made all her sacrifices worth it. She had no regrets and would have done it all over again. Diane Crain was exhausted and watched the girls until they were out of her visual range. She looked at the recliner in front of the fireplace where her husband always sat, turned, and headed for the bedroom to lie down. Suddenly, she was very tired.

**

Chapter Twenty-Three

It was bittersweet, but as Amy went through the daily motions of living, sometimes she felt so close to Aaron, it was as if she could turn around and he would be there and would tell her one of his bad jokes and they would laugh like there was no tomorrow. One of the things she missed the most were the mornings when she would wake up and smell the coffee and there, he was coming towards her with a big smile, and a steaming cup in his hands for her. They were both such chatterboxes. but she loved their talks and sometimes, on occasion, they could talk for hours. She was sure the feeling of his nearness was God's way of getting her through the pain and knew instinctively it was a gift and wouldn't last. The house seemed so empty without him. She couldn't believe it, but she missed the steady hum of his oxygen concentrator. Just as Aaron had hoped, she did go back to singing and writing music. She went on to finish, *Only Heaven Knows My Love for You*, she had started in Aaron's last days, and just as he predicted it skyrocketed to the top and was still number one on the charts.

Coming home after a tour was so hard now. Aaron always called her when she was gone to tell her good night, and she couldn't wait to get home and see him at the end of every tour. Edie had just put Brittany down for bed and after the usual two-drinks of water routine, and back to bed, she was unwinding with a cup of steaming coffee.

"No, no, Beak, Beak, Mine e e e e e e, Brittany screamed as she chased Beacon from the dining room past Edie and they sprinted for the steps, Beacon scrambling for the lead.

"Britany, what in the world? Beacon, come here this minute. What do you have in your mouth? Where did you get that tape?" Drop it. Beacon bowed his head and carefully dropped it into her hand. Young lady, what are you doing out of bed? Where did you get this?"

Brittany immediately took it from Edie's hand and ran towards the television. "Want Mickey Mouse." She giggled.

"No Mickey Mouse, young lady. You're going straight to bed. She jumped up and took Brittany by the hand. It was when she took the tape from Brittany and turned around to put it in the cabinet, that she saw her name written in Aaron's script on the VHS tape. She felt as if her heart would beat out of her chest. Then she noticed the other tapes in disarray where Brittany must have been rooting through them. She couldn't believe there was a second tape lying on its side with Brittany's name on it. She walked to the entertainment center and. put the tape with her name on it into the 8-Track Tape Player.

165

"Daddy," Brittany squealed when she saw Aaron on the screen. Beacon whimpered and lay down at Edie's feet, ears pinned back and visibly upset. Aaron must have made the tape before he got so sick because he looked wonderful. He was so handsome it made her heart ache.

"Hi Sweetheart, I trust God has led you to find this at just the right time. I wish He could have let us grow old together, but I guess it wasn't meant to be. I think I'm still in shock, and trying to process I have the big "C." You know, when we were dating, you asked me once if I knew I only had one day left to live what would I do? I think I laughed it off at the time. If I knew what I know now I would have a completely different answer. My answer would be that I would choose that day to spend loving you, Edie. I want you to know that you have made me the happiest man I have ever been in my life in the short time we've been together. I can't imagine how much harder this is for you being left behind but I'm so grateful that God has given us our beautiful little girl. She was created with so much love. By now you realize I've made a tape for Brittany as well. I trust God will help you choose the exact moment for her to see it. I want you to continue singing. You have such a gift, darling and I'm sure it will help your heart heal. I love you so much and one day we will be together again in heaven. Until then don't ever let anyone or anything steal your dreams. I love you, Edie."

"Mommy, why are you crying? Brittany wrapped her chubby little arms around her mother's neck; Sorry, Mommy, she said patting her face."

"It's okay, honey, Let's get you to bed." Beacon followed them quietly and somberly up the stairs as if he knew things were never going to be the same.

"Mommy, Mommy, I'm a big girl now. I put on my dress all by myself." Brittany's dress wasn't buttoned, and she didn't have a slip on or shoes and socks, but Edie praised her like the big girl she was. Beacon was right behind her, a little greyer and a little slower but forever loyal and dedicated to the role to which he was born. Miso, in typical feline character, napped nearby without a care in the world. For today, God allowed her to feel Aaron's nearness and she embraced it while she could. She knew he wanted her to live a full life and she'd find a way.

The End

Author's Note

I want to thank you for reading *Don't Forget the Butterflies*. Even though Edie and Aaron are fictitious characters, it shows how their love and faith in God healed their wounded souls. Whatever pain we endure and carry through our lives, it is my sincere hope that Edie and Aaron's story reinforces that there isn't anything that love and faith in God cannot conquer. *Don't Forget the Butterflies* is a tribute to my late husband and all the young soldiers who fought in the Vietnam War and the impact it had on their lives. When they returned home, the horrific memories never left them; they had to learn how to live with them. We can only imagine their pain, what they felt, and still do daily.

Wars have continued since and unfortunately will continue to occur but if we are to learn one thing from the horrors of war we can live and love each day like the butterfly. We are only here for a short time. I believe that is the greatest gift we can give one another.

If you enjoyed my book, please drop me an email at my website, creationsbylynn.org so I can notify you when my next book, *The Sword Cuts Both Ways* comes out.

www.ingramcontent.com/pod-product-compliance
Lightning Source LLC
Chambersburg PA
CBHW030549030726
47495CB00004B/1189